~ Sisters: The Karma Twist ~

By Michelle Linn-Gust

CHELLEHEAD WORKS

ISBN: 978-0-9723318-7-6
Library of Congress Control Number: 2011911619

Chellehead Works
info@chelleheadworks.com
505-266-3134 (voice)
Albuquerque, New Mexico

Printed in the United States of America
First Printing September 2011

Designed by Megan Herndon, chalk drawing by Julia Herndon

For J, who unknowingly inspired me
to pick up an unfinished seventeen-year-old manuscript,
recycle it, and start all over again
to make it the story it was supposed to be.

~ Sisters: The Karma Twist ~

TABLE OF CONTENTS

~ Sisters: The Karma Twist ~

"It was Julie's idea, seriously," Katie whispered to Sarah from the middle of the couch where they sat when the mysterious woman walked in.

"Who is she?" Sarah whispered back, not having a clue what was going on. Julie greeted the woman and led her to the dining room table where several others cleared a spot for her. "What's going on?" Sarah wondered why she was the last to know.

Julie walked over to Sarah and held out her hand. "I have someone I want you to meet," she said, her blonde curls falling forward into her face as she leaned over the couch.

"Why me?" Sarah asked looking around. "There are ten other people in the room. Why me?"

"Because in high school you were the only one who we could dare to get her tarot cards read at the county fair so I know you'll be the first to see the psychic." Julie pointed her head toward the woman who was pulling out her deck of cards.

Sarah's mouth dropped open. Katie took the sangria from her hand. "That was high school. That was a long time ago. I'm not that person anymore."

Julie laughed and tugged at Sarah's arm until she relented. When Sarah got up, no one applauded. Instead, they all looked grateful that she was the one going to see the psychic first. Sarah swore she heard a collective sigh among the group as she sat down at the table and Kelly, the psychic, handed her a deck of cards.

Kelly didn't look like the psychic Sarah remembered from that evening at the county fair during their junior year. There was very little she remembered from that night anyway. Julie was right; she had been the one to take the dare and get her tarot cards read. All Sarah remembered caring about was who her husband would be. And here she was in her thirties and still not married. Maybe that's why she didn't remember it. She probably was told there wouldn't be a husband. Now she feared she had been jinxed, shaking the thought from her head as she shuffled the cards, not aware that everyone behind her whispered, wondering what Sarah might be told.

"I'll read the cards in a bit," Kelly said, after Sarah placed them halfway between the two of them on the table. She looked away from Sarah, almost as if she stared at an invisible teleprompter. Sarah watched her, thinking she might recognize her from the grocery store but not as a psychic. She was an average-looking woman with graying long black hair.

"Your sister died?"

Sarah's heart fell. The room gasped behind her. She felt Julie move closer. "Yes," she said, tentatively.

"She tells me that you two had a pre-birth karmic agreement to advance both your souls." Another gasp erupted behind Sarah although she could barely focus on Kelly to understand what she said. Sarah's legs shook under the table. She tried to steady them with her hands but it didn't work. This was too close for comfort. "You are the vehicle in the agreement to help people you've never met."

Sarah's mouth dropped open. But what did that mean? Kelly continued to talk for what seemed like another minute or two. "Your sister says that she's glad you kept her slippers." Sarah didn't think she could ever get her mouth back together.

Kelly reiterated what she said with the cards that Sarah had shuffled. "It seems that the relationship you don't have in your life will come when you finally pursue this job you haven't fulfilled in your agreement."

"What am I supposed to do?" Sarah blurted out. "I don't get it."

Kelly's face stared at the imaginary teleprompter again. "She says you're partway there. The spirit guides will lead you if you let them."

An egg timer on the table dinged and Sarah knew her time ended. Julie hugged her as Sarah walked back to the couch dazed. No one said a word and Julie slipped into the spot to have her reading next.

"Your sister died?" Katie asked when Sarah held her sangria again and sipped it, her hands now shaking.

Sarah nodded her head. "She killed herself when I was in college."

* * * * *

"Jenna," Sarah said to her sister as she lay in bed that night, "why couldn't you give me a message about how much you miss me. Or how you're sorry you killed yourself and missed out in life. Or why couldn't you have told me why you killed yourself." Sarah thought for a moment. It had been a long time since she had spoken to Jenna. For years she had talked to her as if she stood with Sarah but at some point she stopped. She wasn't sure why. Or when. But tonight she needed to. She felt her heart racing.

What was this whole thing about the pre-birth karma agreement anyway? After a few days, Sarah let it go. She had too much to do to think about it. It didn't make any sense to her.

CHAPTER 2

They didn't really understand the game they were going to see. "Your dad got the tickets," their mom kept telling them. "You're going to have a great time with your dad today."

Sarah remembered that first drive to the game, though, how the city engulfed them as they got closer to Wrigleyville, the streets tighter, the number of people increasing. What she wasn't prepared for was the long nothingness in the game.

But maybe it was their dad, too consumed with his beer and peanuts to pay much attention to the girls. What was that their mom had said about having a great time with their dad at the game?

"We should make something up," Sarah whispered, finishing her hot dog and taking a drink from her cup, only ice left.

"Like what?" Jenna asked, a too-big Cubs hat perched on her head.

"Our own baseball game," Sarah suggested.

But just as Sarah said that, they heard the crack of the bat, and the crowd roared. It felt like slow motion as the hands in the park did a wave through the crowd following the ball, a foul for sure now. But everyone wondered–where would it land?

To Sarah's surprise, but more to Jenna's, it bonked Jenna on the head and landed in Sarah's lap. Jenna was too surprised to cry out. Everyone stared at them, including their dumbfounded father.

Later, on the ride home, all he could talk about was how he'd never caught a ball himself. Jenna handed the ball to Sarah and they giggled. There was no reason to make up a game now. Instead, they needed to learn the rules of baseball.

However, that wasn't their first excursion into baseball. Just a few years before, driving home from Niagara Falls, they had stopped in Cooperstown.

"Why didn't you let us go in?" Sarah would ask their mother years later. She shrugged her shoulders, continuing to mold raw meat, egg, and bread crumbs into meatballs. "It was expensive. I didn't see taking you two in for something you wouldn't understand."

"So you let Dad go by himself?" Jenna asked, irritated from her seat at the kitchen table where she was reading the newspaper.

"It was his idea," their mother reminded them. "You'll get there one day. Maybe you should go when Jenna graduates from high school next year. Take a road trip."

"You're suggesting we take a road trip by ourselves to Cooperstown?" Sarah asked, puzzled that their somewhat overprotective mother encouraged them to fly away from the nest. She met Jenna's eyes and they both lit up with big grins.

"We should do it," Jenna said, slapping her hand on the table. "Don't forget you told us we could." She grabbed a piece of paper and pen by the phone and documented what Arlene McCall had just said: "You should go to Cooperstown after Jenna graduates from high school. Take a road trip." Jenna walked over to their mother and stuck it on the counter in front of her. "Mom, please sign this and I'd really like some blood to go with it."

Arlene rolled her eyes, washed her hands, and said, "I'll sign but you're not getting any of my blood."

"Unless you accidentally cut yourself making dinner," Sarah piped in from the other end of the kitchen where she leaned on the pantry door.

Jenna stuck the piece of paper on the front of the refrigerator where it stayed until years later when the house was sold. Sarah had taken it down and placed it in her purse. When she got home that evening she used a Cubs magnet to hang it on her refrigerator door. The note looked a little crusty and wrinkled but the words were clear, as well as Jenna's loopy girlish handwriting.

She still hadn't made it to Cooperstown.

*****

Sarah's eyes darted back and forth across the wall calendar of German Shepherd dogs in her hand. First it was Valentine's Day. Then the start of spring training. Then that date. Every year she did this, looking at the calendar. She placed it on the kitchen counter and let her elbows rest on the cool tile to lament the dates.

It would be ten years this year. That meant ten dozen cookies. What would she do with ten dozen cookies? It was easy those first few years when she could usually eat a dozen. Or up until the seventh year when her parents still lived in the house. But now ten dozen were too many. She let her left hand drop to the counter and tapped her fingers on the white surface. Who would want a portion of her ten dozen oatmeal cookies?

And why was the number ten always so significant? Her friend Julie would be married ten years this year, having married the summer after Jenna died. She and her husband were going on a cruise, sans the kids, to celebrate. It felt like much of life was synchronized in units of ten.

But Sarah stopped thinking about the number ten and focused on the sports section from the newspaper lying on the counter. The reminder about spring training was there although it didn't take much to remind Sarah. At the school where she taught, the baseball kids in her class jogged her memory with their grade checks for their athletic eligibility.

She flattened her palm against the counter. School. She could take the oatmeal cookies to school.

It was going to take a lot of butter to make ten dozen oatmeal cookies, she thought, as she made up the grocery list. There was no written recipe. Sarah would never forget this recipe she and Jenna had memorized and then tweaked starting in Sarah's early high school days. During the years she sometimes recited it in her head when she needed something to focus on, thinking about butter, eggs, sugar, vanilla, then flour and oats. It was enough to keep her mind busy at least for a few minutes. And it kept her focused on Jenna. Or not forgetting Jenna and something they had shared.

Writing the necessary ingredients on her grocery list along with salmon, milk, and lettuce was another story. Her mind wandered back to the sports section. She wondered why spring training that year hadn't been enough to keep Jenna from ending her life. What was different that year? Baseball had been integral for both of them for many years. They celebrated the start of the season and mourned it when it ended with the fall classic, The World Series. For ten years, Sarah had never found an answer.

She placed the grocery the list on the refrigerator and walked into the living room where her German Shepherd Mairzy snored loudly on the couch. Mairzy opened one eye as Sarah walked by then slowly closed it.

Sarah stared out her front window. There never would be any answers. She knew that now. But sometimes she just longed for a conversation over cookie dough. And making ten dozen cookies was the closest she could get to that. It was the only time all year that she truly felt Jenna with her.

*****

Who was Jenna? No one asked her anymore. She missed talking about her sister. There were nearly four years between them, the perfect number, her mother said, because she didn't have two kids in diapers or going through the same developmental stages at the same time. Her father said it meant there only would be one year that they would overlap with college tuition bills, hinting to Sarah to not take more than four years to graduate. Their older brother Matt was five years older than Sarah, leaving a large span between him and Jenna.

Matt was long off doing his own thing with his friends when Jenna came along. He didn't play with them as they all grew older, mostly taunting them by hitting them in the back with his nerf football or skateboarding past them on the driveway while they roller skated away from his constant attacks. He grunted at the dinner table when asked how his day went, his sisters staring at him, wishing he'd talk and acknowledge them. They often poked their heads in his room, filled with sports posters, and wished they knew the brother who ignored them. But that never changed.

Sarah remembered how she and her sister played together. And some days she only remembered the good.

Most of all, she remembered that Jenna bled red and royal blue.

Sometimes Sarah wanted to prick her vein. She wondered if people would think she too wanted to kill herself and was always afraid to try. Her rationale to herself was to find out if she still bled red and royal blue even without Jenna around. But part of her thought maybe she wanted to do it to make sure she was still alive, that she still felt anything. That when she finally worked up the courage to prick herself, she would jump backward from the nerve reaction and watch her finger begin to bleed. No one understood when she tried to explain it to friends who only stared at her, their faces blank as a new sheet of paper.

It hurt that even in her family there was such a lack of understanding. Sarah knew they all did the best they could, giving each other space almost to the point of tiptoeing around each other at times. Sarah wanted to talk about Jenna but she feared, as she sat at the breakfast table that summer after Jenna died, eating the pancakes her mother made for her, that it would send her mother running out of the room in tears. Or her father to start crying. And Matt was a whole different animal. He never came home nor did he call and check on them, their mother frustrated to only get his wife on the phone who would insist she would make him call. But he didn't.

The following year after Jenna died, Sarah's graduation from Wisconsin had been difficult. Her parents drove up and when the graduation ceremony ended, all of them stifled in sadness even on such a happy day, they gathered her bags and boxes of stuff, packed them in the car, and Sarah cried her way back home behind her sunglasses with her favorite lamp and stuffed animals sitting next to her. She felt as though "Pomp & Circumstance" had been stolen from her. Jenna was supposed to be there. Sarah knew Jenna would have decorated the apartment, wanted to hold a party, wouldn't have let them go home until they had "appropriately" celebrated Sarah's graduation.

"It means we're fifty percent to the bakery," Sarah knew Jenna would say because Sarah had graduated from college. Once Jenna graduated from college they would be one hundred percent to the bakery. College graduations meant they'd removed a large obstacle from their paths. Jenna never got there.

Each time Sarah struggled in school, feeling overwhelmed, it was Jenna who would call and root her on. "You can't give up. You're fifty percent of the bakery," she would say, as if really saying, "Duh!"

Sarah's graduation party the next weekend was no better. It was the first time the whole family had gathered since Jenna's funeral: her grandparents, cousins, aunts, uncles, and her brother. Matt didn't talk much. Why would it be any different now? Secretly, she hoped it would but the reality side of her told her it always would be the same. She tried to let the expectation go.

Everyone insisted she open her gifts, something she really didn't want to do around the crowd. Something wasn't right about all this attention. She knew she'd give up everything to have her sister back, to have her be part of this family event. To be part of Sarah's life again.

Sarah sat in a webbed lawn chair, flanked on each side by a grandmother. "I'm so glad you finished school," each one said, lamenting her own experiences. "Now you can have a boyfriend." The stack of gifts was placed in front of Sarah by her younger cousins who only cared about what was in the brightly wrapped packages. But it was the one from Matt that made her glad once again she wore sunglasses.

Sarah had no idea what it was, tugging at the ribbon, knowing his wife Donna wrapped it and did all the work although Matt probably told her what to get. But as soon as she tore a corner off the wrapping paper, she saw part of the logo. A Cubs t-shirt.

"Not just any t-shirt," Matt said, pointing his beer bottle at her, "the T-shirt for this season."

Sarah forced a smile on her face as she shook it open and held it up against herself for everyone to see. They Ooohed and Ahhhhed. She whispered thanks. "Your favorite team," her cousin Tim said. "My favorite team, too." Sarah continued to force the smile.

Had everyone forgotten? She wondered. She could barely listen to the crack of a bat. She couldn't bear to hear Harry Caray's voice. She didn't go near WGN or entertain the thought of buying tickets. It was too hard without Jenna. There would be no more frozen yogurt runs. No more oatmeal cookies. No frozen yogurt cookie sandwiches for their treats during the games.

And she knew she could never say this to her brother; she could never tell him that everything had changed now that Jenna was gone, and baseball didn't have the same meaning to her. The relationship that bound them together didn't have it in the contract. And what about her parents? What would they say? "Well, you don't expect everyone to know what you want and don't want, do you?"

Now she thanked everyone, thanked them for gifts that didn't mean much. She didn't want anything but for her sister to come back and no one could accomplish that. She knew they tried, they wanted to help her.

They thought maybe the gifts might be a reason for her to smile. But no one really knew.

*****

Faith always had been a struggle for Sarah. While Jenna learned the Apostle's Creed and the Beatitudes with ease, seemingly enjoying and understanding them along the way, Sarah relied on rote memorization for something she knew she would never remember in the future. Or care about after she was tested on it. Jenna loved to go to church even when they were young and fidgety. And the once-a-year day when they traveled into the city to the cemetery where all the relatives were buried, Jenna was right there, holding their grandmother's hand as she explained about who each of the gravestones represented: all the relatives who came from Eastern Europe and their stories of struggle to provide for their families in the new world.

To Sarah, the church revolved around death. She didn't find hope there. As she grew up, dragged to Sunday Mass, she felt it was about people and their fear of death. They went to church to make sure that death wouldn't be bad and to be told that Heaven was this great place they all would eventually visit. All Sarah could think was she was in no hurry to get there.

After Jenna died, Sarah began to wonder if her sister's comfort with death was a reason she could end her life. Maybe she felt comforted that all the relatives had gone before her would be waiting to greet her. That their grandfather would be there to see her. And Nellie, the dog they'd had as kids, would be wagging her tail when she arrived. Maybe her fear of what life held dissipated with the thought that everyone would be there to greet her, although probably confused she arrived much too young. Of course maybe that didn't matter once one showed up in the afterlife.

While in college though, Sarah had found a need to pray. She couldn't pinpoint exactly what caused it. Or did something have to cause it? Couldn't she wake up one day and realize she felt a need to have hope for her world and the world that circled around her? Every night, lulling herself to sleep, she prayed for her family, for everyone to be happy, and for peace in the world. She remembered how her aunt once told her that she had a long list of people she prayed for each night. Sarah couldn't figure out how she could stay awake long enough. Often Sarah would wake up several hours later, realizing she had never finished the prayer.

Sitting in church, Jenna's casket at the front, Sarah wondered why she had bothered with all those prayers. What had she been praying for anyway? She didn't understand at the time that maybe Jenna was happy to leave the world for the next one. Perhaps Jenna felt relief of ending her present life. All Sarah could think about was what she had lost. What her family had lost. What the world had lost without Jenna. She couldn't begin to comprehend that as Jenna placed the phone cord around her neck, she wasn't thinking about anyone else, just herself and her pain. She couldn't think about any plans she and Sarah had made. She couldn't think about her hope for the future. She could only see several feet in front of her and all those feet consumed her with mental pain.

Sarah wondered, not listening to the priest, barely able to follow along with anything since Jenna died, how God would let Jenna end her life. People often discussed why God let bad things happen to people. The church taught them all about sacrifice. But Sarah didn't buy any of it. She didn't even have an answer to what she thought death was. She just knew that she didn't get it and that meant she'd push it away.

She quit praying that day. No use, she thought. If she couldn't keep Jenna there with her prayers, then what was the point of praying for anything else?

*****

Sarah always wished for Jenna's hair. She never told anyone. Not even Jenna. For all the things they discussed, which until Jenna died, Sarah thought there was very little they never talked about, it was one of the few things Sarah never told her sister. Jenna had thick blonde hair that when grown long could hold curl better than anything Sarah could imagine than her own limp brownish black mop. Sarah watched Jenna curl her hair, and do it with ease. She hardly tried with her own hair, embarrassed about what it would look like when it flopped from the humidity in the air.

"Arggh," Jenna would complain though. "It's too thick to get a comb through it. Sometimes I think I might have lost a pencil in there."

Down the hall in her room, Sarah would laugh while she attempted to finish an English paper while Jenna fought with the curling iron. She didn't care if Jenna complained. She still wished for that thick hair. As Jenna lay in her casket on that morning of the funeral, Sarah touched her sister's hair. It was different, like one of those model heads they had to play with growing up. It almost felt as if it wasn't Jenna's anymore because Jenna had moved on. She looked peaceful, her green eyes shut to the world that gave her fear and pain no one understood.

Jenna was a swimmer. While Jenna wasn't the thinnest girl in the world, she held bread and pasta better on her body than most people. Jenna could down half a pizza while Sarah only could eat two pieces. Her tennis skirt reminded her there wasn't room for error. Jenna's swimsuit never looked too small.

Mostly though, Jenna was happy. Or so everyone thought. At the funeral, Sarah talked to what felt like endless people about how happy Jenna had looked that last day at school. Why had her smiles hid so much pain? What was that pain anyway? And her mother would run into people at the grocery store, at the library, anywhere in town, and they would stop and tell Arlene McCall they couldn't believe Jenna had died. "We always thought she was such a happy girl."

That's when Sarah began to read up on what suicide was. The act of killing oneself. But why would one kill oneself? What led to that point? Obviously from what everyone said, if she was such a happy person, then was it possible a happy person could die by suicide?

There was only one suicide in Sarah's life before Jenna. It was their second cousin Rick. She only remembered him from a few family gatherings and most of that was vague. He was a tall skinny guy, almost ten years older than Sarah. He stared at them when they were introduced. Sometimes she heard her mother, her sisters, and her grandmother discussing Rick. She knew that's whom they talked about because their voices hushed as if Rick himself might hear them.

"I heard he was back in rehab again," Grandma Vincent would say. "I don't know how they deal with him."

Then one day he went in the basement of his parents' house and shot himself. Rick was never spoken of again. Sarah didn't remember there being a funeral. If there had been one, her mother hadn't gone. Rick was her mother's cousin, Charlotte's son, and the gist of the story said he was "never quite right." As he got older, he found his way into drugs and alcohol. The hushed discussions ranged from drug rehab to arrests to finally a bipolar diagnosis.

That was the type of person Sarah thought died by suicide. Not happy-go-lucky Jenna. Not the sister who she had plans with for the future. Suicide was about the people who visibly struggled with life and everyone saw it. No one saw or heard Jenna's struggles. The more she read, the more she understood that Jenna wasn't so far out of the ordinary though. For whatever reason, she kept her pain within her, not unlike others who have ended their lives, Sarah learned.

She bit her nail. Surely there were warning signs that others saw. Maybe she didn't because she was away. Someone had to know something though. Sarah wasn't quite sure where to start.

CHAPTER 3

"There's no butter," Jenna sighed, her head shoved into the refrigerator in their parents' kitchen.

"There must be some margarine," Sarah said, feeling somewhat impatient now that the other ingredients rested on the white counter. "There's no way. How could we be out?"

"We are," Jenna sighed, standing back up and facing her sister as she closed the door. She shrugged her shoulders. "Sounds like a grocery store run to me."

Sarah looked at the kitchen clock on the oven. "We better hurry or we won't have any cookies at the start of the game."

They climbed into the family station wagon, Jenna turning up the music while Sarah backed the car out of the driveway into the Midwest June evening air. The lightning bugs had begun to blink in the night and the girls would try to catch them on their way back into the house, the butter in Jenna's hand.

Sarah loved to think about those nights with Jenna even though she had been gone ten years. She knew she clung to them because it felt as each year went by, a little of Jenna's life faded into the background. Jenna remained eighteen while Sarah now advanced into her thirties. She continued to grow her life yet there remained just a finite amount of memories of life with Jenna.

The idea of losing what she had left scared Sarah. She compensated by spending a little time each week, when she was driving or standing in a line, remembering who her sister was. Still, she wished she could share Jenna's life with others although she was never sure who. A part of her longed to be in contact with Jenna's friends, to hear their memories, to know they still talked about her and what she had brought to their lives.

*****

Going home that day, the day that Jenna had died, was the worst day of Sarah's life. She could still say that despite the ten years that had gone by. Her worst day teaching, her worst day coaching, her worst day because she wished she hadn't gotten out of bed, still didn't compare to the phone call and the subsequent trip back to Cedarville.

By the time Sarah got there it was dark and the majority of people had come and gone. Jenna's body had been long removed and the door to her room shut. After everyone greeted Sarah, the relatives left, and her parents went back to the kitchen, leaving her on her own. She took her bag upstairs, the bag filled with the outfit she wasn't sure she wanted to wear to her sister's funeral. Heck, she didn't know what to wear to Jenna's funeral. It was an event she was never supposed to attend.

She walked into the bathroom, thinking only of the fact that she had to use the bathroom, when the sight of Jenna's toothbrush, and the toothpaste rolled up next to it, set off Sarah's tears. She tried not to look at herself in the mirror. She'd been crying on and off all day and didn't want to see how red her eyes looked. She didn't expect that something so routine about their daily lives would send her back to tears. It wasn't taking much. She still couldn't believe that Jenna was dead. She didn't think part of her would believe it until she saw her body at the funeral home.

As she stood there at the sink crying, she heard a knock at the door and a male voice. "Are you okay, Sarah?" Matt.

Sarah looked for a tissue to wipe her eyes and then opened the door. She knew it was okay to cry for anyone and anything but something made her rinse her face in cool water. Maybe it was for her rather than anyone else.

Her older brother stood in the doorway looking like he had been crying, too. He held his arms open and Sarah walked into them, not having anywhere else to go since he was blocking the entire doorway.

It wasn't a comfortable hug. They were never close. Sarah wasn't sure why he hugged her. Maybe he felt obligated. She thought it felt stiff and forced. Or maybe that's the way he was with Donna. Matt had never been part of her life. She wondered why he would want to be now. No, that didn't sound right. She knew she should be more grateful that her brother reached out to her. She thought it would be short lived. And it was.

As Sarah lay in bed that first night, she couldn't sleep even though she felt bathed in exhaustion. She had no clue what lay ahead of her. She couldn't think about what was ahead. She felt stuck in the present moment, her thoughts stuck on comprehending that Jenna had died. Her brain tried to understand where Jenna was.

All those years of CCD, all the classes, all the prayers, all that Jenna had loved to learn about life and the joy it could bring. None of it had been enough because Jenna killed herself, something they had been taught was a sin. All that talk about purgatory. They never knew it was a place in Colorado where people skied. No, it was about where you ended up when you took your life at your own hand. Wasn't that what suicide meant?

Sarah rolled over. She wished she could sleep. She wished she could rest her mind for a few hours. She didn't want to think anymore. She wanted to turn it off. The house was almost too quiet. Matt was down the hall in his old room, now the guestroom, and she was in hers. The only person missing to complete their family was Jenna.

Sitting up, Sarah decided it wasn't worth it. She tiptoed down the hall and slipped into Jenna's bed. She didn't care that several hours ago in that room her sister had ended her life. She didn't care that a slew of people had been in the room throughout the day. She only wanted to be close to her sister.

There were many nights where they were inseparable. When they were younger, Arlene McCall often sighed when she found them in bed together in the morning. "I should have let you two share a room," she said, although she would be glad she didn't during their early adolescence when they didn't get along. Sarah admitted that during those years there were times when she never thought she and Jenna would get along again. They couldn't agree on anything and their father often had each one by the arm on either side of him. "Get it together, girls," he would seethe. "I know you don't like each other but you're still family."

When was it that it changed? Sarah wondered. When she entered high school was the best she could tell. Then they could watch baseball together again. That's when they began to make the cookies. Their relationship transformed into something else, something greater and more special than it had been before.

They told stories into the night, but mostly they talked about their goals and dreams. That was how the dream of the bakery began, late one night when they'd already been told once to go to sleep. Instead, it was 1:00 in the morning and they couldn't stop dreaming about the place where they would endlessly bake cookies and make people happy just because they fed them great cookies. "But we should probably serve cakes, too," Jenna added. Sarah always thought her sister was a better dreamer than she was. Sarah was better on the math end; she could ace the business problems, but Jenna was the creative one.

Just that morning, Jenna had been in that bed. Sarah hadn't slept in Jenna's bed in awhile though. Being away at school changed things as it again would have the next year when Jenna went to a college she hadn't chosen yet. But there had been many nights when she'd been home on breaks where they stayed up talking, Jenna asking about college and boys and how Sarah's degree was coming along because she needed that degree for their bakery. And then Sarah would ask Jenna the same questions about school, boys, and where she was thinking about going to college.

Now Sarah realized those conversations would never happen again. Sarah only could have them with herself. How could there be no Jenna? It didn't seem possible. She felt a tear slide down her face and hit the pillowcase; Jenna's purple pillowcase that she would never use again.

No one knew about the bakery. It had been their secret. When their parents asked Sarah why she was majoring in nutrition and business, she told them it was because she thought she might have a consulting business. Truth was she had liked the idea of helping people with their food selections and diets. She looked into other ways of making cookies. She told Jenna that maybe they could cut down on the butter using something else, like applesauce, and still offer a great product but one that wasn't so fattening.

"No way," Jenna would challenge her from the mixer where they'd be working in the kitchen. "You don't mess with a good thing. Who wants a low-fat cookie?" she asked, pointing at their mother's box of low-calorie chocolate cookies. "Have you ever tried one of those pieces of crap Mom buys?" She turned up her nose.

Sarah let Jenna talk. She knew she'd have time to change her mind. After all, part of the bakery could be devoted to these items. Not the whole bakery. Jenna was missing the cookies for the cakes. But now that wouldn't happen.

The tears wore Sarah out and she finally found sleep.

*****

~ Sisters: The Karma Twist ~

They said that it was traumatic sometimes to recall the experience of learning that a loved one had died by suicide. Sarah thought of her mother finding Jenna hanging in her closet from the phone cord, an extra one that had been in the tool drawer in the kitchen. She had to search for it, they all knew. It wasn't easily found and it had been there for years. Sarah herself had been at class when her sister died. She always wondered if she had a funny feeling when Jenna died because they had been so close. More than anything, she remembered the exhaustion she felt that day.

CHAPTER 4

Reentry. The only time Sarah thought of that word was in conjunction with the space program. Moon landings. The reentry to the earth. But she never thought of it in terms of her reentry back at college. Until she was faced with it.

The car packed, Sarah stood with the keys in her hands, her parents in front of her, Arlene McCall's hands filled with rumpled tissues. Sarah didn't want to say anything but she thought maybe her mother should carry around the entire box. Matt had gone home already and just Aunt Martha and Uncle Joe were left in the house, staying a few more days before returning to Minnesota.

The sun had come out for the first time since Jenna died. It was as if enough tears had fallen, enough gray had covered the sky, and now it was time for life to begin again. The problem was Sarah didn't want to begin life again. She was exhausted and glad her friend Maria had come with her from school to attend Jenna's funeral. At least she had company for the drive back to Madison. She wanted to turn the music up loud on the radio and pretend for a little while that everything was okay.

"I wish you wouldn't leave," her mother said, her eyes filling with tears again. Sarah didn't want to hug her anymore. She was tired of being hugged. She didn't want anyone to touch her. "But I know you need to go."

I need normalcy, she wanted to shout to anyone who would listen. Life had changed but she wasn't so sure she was ready to accept that change.

The next morning she returned to class. Her professors had been informed and were immediately at her side when she walked in the door. "You know you don't have to be here," they said, repeating each other over the next few days as she ventured to all her classes. "You know you can have some time off."

"I want to be here," Sarah said, unable to explain to them why. She wanted life to go on as it had. She wanted to cling to whatever was left of her old life. She didn't know if she was going to completely lose the rest of her old life. She felt like she was hanging onto a light pole in the midst of the storm, as if that's all she had.

There was little reprieve in that time. Sarah walked around in a daze. She didn't remember much of those first weeks. Somewhere someone had told her that there would be a lot of shock. Her body adjusted to the blow that her sister was gone. And not returning.

Prior to Jenna's death, she and her roommates had planned a party for that first weekend after Jenna's death. "We were going to have it while you were gone but we thought that was disrespectful," they said when she returned.

Sarah stared at them. She was glad. Yes, she was glad they didn't do it without her, while she was burying her sister and being hugged by cousins she'd never met. But what about the party they still planned to have? How could she attend a party? And she would have to. It was going to be at their apartment.

"So we rescheduled it for this coming Saturday night." Three sets of eyes watched her. "Are you okay with that?"

Sarah, who sat in the oversized chair on the other side of the room, could only stare at her roommates. She knew they meant well. And she wanted to be back at school. But a party? How could she do a party?

"Look, you can disappear any time you want during it," Celia said, holding her hand out. "We totally get it and everyone else will."

"I-I-I…," Sarah said, shaking her head. She didn't know what to say. She got up and left the room, shutting the door behind her. She didn't shut it hard, just enough to let them know she wanted to be left alone.

She knew they would leave her alone only because they didn't know what else to do with her.

Throwing parties had been one of the best parts about the four girls renting an apartment together. While Sarah wouldn't say she was much of a party girl, the parties they held weren't about drinking so much as endless rounds of Uno and potato chips. And that next Saturday night was no exception.

Sarah stood in the kitchen as everyone arrived, busying herself making her mother's famous spinach dip. "Hey Sarah," her friends greeted her awkwardly. Some hugged her, some placed a hand on her shoulder. But all of them said, "We're really sorry about your sister."

Sarah kept smiling as she mixed the dip, probably over mixed at that point. But she couldn't stop. She was afraid if she stopped mixing the dip, she might begin to cry. Finally, Brenda removed it from her hands gently. "I think we need to start eating."

She sat down on a couch to watch the Uno game that began, begging out of it, knowing she couldn't focus long enough but not wanting to admit it. They would leave her alone, she knew. No one would beg her to play. But after awhile she found herself getting lost in the jokes, the stories, the goofiness that usually came with them on Saturday nights. It was good to focus on something other than Jenna's death. She ate. She laughed. And finally she played Uno.

But about halfway through the game she felt something weird. "Are you okay?" Celia asked, poking her. "It's your turn, you know."

Sarah tried to shake out of her trance and look for a card to put down. She realized she felt guilty for laughing, for having a good time. She felt guilty for being there without Jenna. After all, Jenna was dead; how could she be having a good time? Wasn't she supposed to mourn and be sad for a year after her sister's death? What was that year of mourning gig?

She felt confused and struggled to finish the game, begging off to her room when she was done, curling up under her comforter and wishing there was an easier way to cope with the road ahead of her. The road she didn't understand.

*****

It was a Thursday and school was kicking her butt to put it mildly. They were a month in and she was already trying to figure out how she would survive the rest of the semester with eighteen hours, including one lab. She wasn't even sure she'd get home for spring break although she knew she couldn't break tradition. She and Jenna always watched spring training games on television. They hadn't been able to convince their dad to take them to Phoenix.

"We'll just go every year after I get into college," Jenna had pledged, teasing their dad.

"After you turn twenty-one," he always would add.

"Sarah will be twenty-one before me," Jenna would tease again.

Frank McCall would playfully push Jenna away. Those were the moments they joked about through the years. "Remember when Dad said I had to be twenty-one before we could go to spring training?" they would ask each other as if it was the funniest thing in the world.

CHAPTER 5

There were parts of Jenna that Sarah forgot after her sister died. She didn't understand why she forgot them. Was it because Jenna wasn't there to remind her with her funny sayings or silly actions? Or was it because the grief covered them up? For several years, she forgot how much she and Jenna shared as high school athletes. Even when Sarah began coaching, her relationship with her sister felt distant, a part of her past that she didn't think she would ever retrieve. A part of her past she didn't think she *could* ever retrieve.

She forgot the mornings she drove Jenna to school, long before the sun was up, for swim practice, returning home for a little more sleep before driving back to school to start classes. Because swimming and tennis both were fall sports, they shared a ride home, something Jenna loved when she was a freshman and Sarah was a senior. She bragged about never having to ride the bus or having to be picked up by their mom like Sarah before she could drive.

It wasn't just those daily moments they shared though. There were the Saturdays, filled with meets and tennis matches, their parents switching off whom they supported each weekend, and the girls gathering with their friends on Saturday nights at the house, Arlene cooking up large stacks of pancakes to keep the girls and later, their boyfriends, full after a long day of competition.

Even after everyone had gone home though, Jenna would find her way into her sister's bed. "How'd it go today?" Sarah would ask, already half asleep when her sister, who took longer than anyone she knew to get ready for bed, finally joined her. "And get your cold feet off my warm feet."

"Why are your feet so warm?" Jenna would giggle, hoping for a response from her sister who would playfully whack her across the head.

"Go to sleep," Sarah would say, yawning. "We can talk in the morning if you're going to keep your cold feet on mine."

"I want to talk now," Jenna would finally relent, pulling her feet off her sister's. "It was hard. I didn't think I could finish that last lap. But I remembered what you told me about staying strong, about how when you think you can't hit another ball, you think of each muscle and focus on making them work." She felt Jenna turn toward her and Sarah opened her eyes, staring at the ceiling, listening to her sister.

"And it helped?"

"Oh my God, did it ever!" Jenna laughed. "I surged to the finish. Coach Thompson said if I could finish that strong then I definitely had more to give off in the middle of the race."

Sarah smiled, feeling a sense of accomplishment for having helped her sister.

"Next weekend, I'm thinking I need to remember that earlier in the race. I'm not sure how fast I can go but maybe it'll help me get my best time yet."

There were many nights when the two girls talked until one fell asleep, the other quietly leaving the room for her own bed. When Sarah went to college, she missed those conversations even though her tennis career had ended with the state tournament her senior year. She missed hearing her sister's voice as the last noise in the darkness before she drifted off to sleep. Most of all, she just missed Jenna.

She often wondered if it was silly or weird that she missed her sister that much. After Jenna died, she didn't have access to other sisters who were in her situation. She yearned to reach out to someone else who understood her situation. No one did though. Not even her own family. She also realized that none of them knew much about those late nights she and Jenna talked together. Matt had long moved out by then and her parents joked how they were lucky if they could stay awake to 10:00 pm.

Sarah wanted to know her sister was nearby. She began to read books by people who felt their loved ones' presence. Some people saw them or heard them. Sarah never felt any of that. Sometimes she let the silence of her room engulf her, hoping that in the deadness of it she might feel her sister. She didn't. And then at some point she gave up. All she had were the memories and she clung to those. It was as if she held a bag in her hand and clutched it close to her chest because she feared someone would steal it from her.

That emptiness took several years to subside. And when it did, Sarah believed it was because of the girls she coached. She didn't feel it so much in teaching during the day but when she got on the court with her girls in the afternoon, often playing against them, or spending time learning about their lives, she felt something come alive inside her again. The longing to be a part of something, like the sisterhood she had shared with Jenna, was replaced with leading a team of girls playing tennis. While Sarah continued to play recreationally, it wasn't the same, and when she got out on the court with them in their matching skirts and listened to the ball thud against the court itself, she could smile. She was home.

While she didn't realize it, the girls sensed something about her, too. They began to come to her with their problems, mostly their struggles in relationships, whether it was their families, their friends, or the boys they liked. Sarah wished for Jenna at those times because she always felt Jenna could dissect those relationships, even as a high school student, better than Sarah. Sarah often felt her sister would have been great in the bakery doing something they could call "counter therapy" as well.

"You should get a dual degree in business and psychology," she would tell her sister. Jenna stuck out her tongue. "No way am I going more than four years. You get the psychology degree along with nutrition and business."

Instead, Sarah helped the girls alone. Often she found herself wondering, what would Jenna do? Even though she didn't feel Jenna with her, she would silently ask for her help. Somehow she had to be there, Sarah would reason with herself. All those people she read about and their stories, surely they were true. People didn't make up that stuff. Why couldn't she sense Jenna with her though?

CHAPTER 6

"Did you really make these?" A voice jolted Sarah away from the paper she was grading. She slapped her hands, one with a pen secured in her fingers, on her desk. She knew better than to allow herself to get carried away with thoughts and memories at her desk. It was a safety issue. When she finally looked up, Mark Lennon, a fellow teacher, stood in the doorway.

Sarah took a deep breath and let a sigh slip out of her mouth. "Yes, I really made them. Did you think I couldn't use my kitchen?"

He smiled, walking further into her room and settling himself on top of one of the student desks. Before taking another bite of the cookie in his hand, he said, "I'd like to do a fundraiser for the baseball team. Do you think you could make me a whole lot of these?"

Sarah's stomach jumped. It was one day past the anniversary of Jenna's death. She peered closer at the man she had never taken much notice of other than they taught at the same school. She made it a point to not follow the baseball team. His life, she assumed, revolved around both baseball and teaching history. "Um, like how many are you talking about? You know I have a teaching job." She pointed at the terribly written quizzes she graded about Aldous Huxley's *Brave New World*.

He thought for a minute, and as he did, Sarah wondered why he never wore a tie. He always dressed well, navy or khaki pants with a white shirt. She pictured the inside of his closet lined with perfectly ironed shirts and pants. It wouldn't take long to arrange them by color. She bit her lip to keep from laughing.

"How about fifty dozen?" he asked, finishing off the cookie. "And we'll reimburse you for the expenses."

Sarah's mouth dropped. How was she going to make fifty dozen cookies in her kitchen? "What are you going to make off my cookies?" she asked finally.

He shrugged his shoulders and ran his hand through his thick brown hair. "We can sell them for $1 each. We'll make $600 minus what we owe you. That will be enough to buy the team t-shirts for this year."

Sarah didn't want to do it. But she had no justified reason to say no. And it was one of those moments where she wished Jenna was there. Even ten years later, she still talked to Jenna, wondered how Jenna would react to things (How much would they email? Leave each other stupid messages on their cell phones?). Yet she never felt that Jenna was with her, except in some way on the anniversary of the day she died, the only day of the year when Sarah made the cookies. And now she was being asked to do it more than once this year.

Tapping her pen, she wished Mark would leave. She wanted to talk to Jenna. She needed some help, some advice. Somehow Jenna had to give her the answers. It never occurred to her that Jenna might be behind bringing Mark to her.

"When do you need the cookies?"

"How about two weeks? We could have them for the opening home game." She looked at her calendar and started to write it down. She had to reconfigure her calculations from this past week and the ten dozen. She wondered what it would be on the fiftieth anniversary of Jenna's death, to make fifty dozen cookies. She'd have to keep the calculations for that day.

"I was wondering if maybe you could add the logo in blue and gold, too?"

"Um, you don't decorate oatmeal cookies," Sarah told Mark shaking her pen at him. "They'll look weird with a Falcon that won't be straight because of the oats and the raisins.

Mark shrugged his shoulders. "I think it'll look great. Why don't you sell these anyway? That's the best oatmeal cookie I've ever had."

"Thank you," Sarah said smugly. "I had a lot of practice."

That afternoon as Sarah drove home after school, she couldn't stop thinking about Mark Lennon. She wondered about him. They had only met once or twice before. She knew he was the new baseball coach, the last one having been fired for having an "inappropriate" relationship with one of the girls on the softball team. Sarah didn't know either one and was grateful for that lack of knowledge. In her five years at the school, she'd gotten her tennis team to sectionals four times and won it twice. She thought the old baseball coach had been a creepy, kind of a slimy guy who didn't have a clue, and maybe that tainted her on all high school baseball coaches.

Girls tennis was a fall sport which she loved. Fall always was such a great time of year. She loved the start of school. Everything was new. Before they went to the computers, her grade books were new. But even now at least her class lists were new. Her girls always came off a strong summer of training and competing. The kids were excited to be back in school unlike after the winter break when they came back depressed by the snow and the cold, waiting for spring fever to hit, and then wanting outside. Spring represented renewal after those long winters. For some reason Jenna stopped seeing that the winter before she died.

But this wasn't about tennis. She'd have to wait to find out more about Mark Lennon.

*****

St. Theresa's Catholic Church stands almost in the center of Cedarville surrounded by old buildings that formed the town in its infancy. It's just three blocks from where Sarah and Jenna attended elementary school. And to the south of the church is the school where they traipsed every Tuesday afternoon during the school year for their Catechism classes. Sarah took a deep breath before she walked into the church.

Sarah's friend Barbara had been married there. And now Julie's kids were being baptized in the same place that Sarah remembered poking her sister almost every Sunday in church as they traveled through childhood.

And it was the place for Jenna's burial Mass. As Sarah stood in the back of the church, now ten years later, waiting for Julie's family to arrive for the baptism of their latest baby, Joey, she watched the landscape in front of her. All those years the view of the steps below her, of the parking lot across the street, had represented Easter, Christmas, and everything in between. The signs of spring at Easter with their pastel dresses; the shoveled snow and the concrete covered with salt to keep everyone from slipping in the darkness of Christmas Eve.

On the day of Jenna's funeral though, Sarah stood in nearly the same place in the church and watched Jenna's casket carried from the hearse into the church by her brother and their cousins. Sarah knew then the church would never have the same meaning to her. She didn't care what her grandmother said in between recitations of her rosary, that they had to pray for Jenna to make sure she made it to Heaven. Sarah knew she was there. She wasn't going to argue with anyone about it. She didn't believe that she had to pray Jenna's way there.

The creaky floors reminded her of their yearly catechism trip across the street from the school to the church to ask for forgiveness of their sins, the wood pews that always looked newly polished, and the darkness of the old church only penetrated by the stained-glass windows and the candles lit on each side of the altar, the very place where their mother often stopped, the girls in tow, to light a candle for someone. She never told them who nor did they ask.

Sarah was sure her mother made more trips to the church since Jenna died. There was little that brought any of them comfort but she knew lighting candles brought comfort for her mother.

And as she waited for Julie's family, Sarah walked to the front of the church, the familiar floor creaking under her feet, a sound that always would remind her of church and if a church didn't have that sound, she didn't believe it could be a church. She stood in front of the rows of votives, few lit since it was early in the day, and tried to remember her mother's routine.

Lighting a candle, leaving a few dollars, she thought of Jenna as she did it. She stood there for a moment, wondering exactly what she should ask for. Sarah knew Jenna was okay and she knew she was in Heaven. It wasn't about Jenna today, she thought.

Instead, she said silently, "Help me, Jenna."

The karma agreement never occurred to her. She had long forgotten about the tarot cards. She still wasn't in an emotional place where she could connect the reading to her sister.

Looking up at the statue of Mary in front of her, Sarah replaced what she saw in front of her with Jenna's face. The sound of a baby crying disrupted her thoughts and she let them go, turning to see the Brown family had arrived.

CHAPTER 7

Sarah loved those cold Friday nights of her childhood. In high school, if there wasn't anything going on, like a football or basketball game, sometimes she and/or Jenna would each have a friend over. Or it would just be the two of them. Sometimes they made cookies. Once or twice they tried chocolate chip, hoping to do something different. Their parents and friends raved about them.

But the girls shrugged their shoulders and returned to the oatmeal. No matter how many recipes they tried, they found their favorite was still based on the one that came off the back of the package of oats itself. They had altered it here and there, changed a pinch or a dash, but the basic recipe remained. They wouldn't swap that stick of butter for anything else though.

Spring represented something different. March meant a lot of cold rain, the kind that made the ground muddy under the dormant grass. Tennis was over. Swimming was over. Neither girl was interested in track. And so they spent the spring mostly at home, gearing up for the summer and the start of tennis and swimming all over again.

It was on a March Friday night during Sarah's senior year that Jenna's cracks began to show. There still was no baseball to watch but the girls had discovered a show about a group of lifeguards in Southern California they found somewhat interesting. "Baywatch" was on each Friday night. Several years before it had been "Miami Vice." The black and white television in their parents' bedroom had graduated to a color one when Frank McCall bought an updated color one for the family room. He and Arlene watched a movie downstairs, on separate couches no less, the two girls content on their own upstairs in the master bedroom haven watching the sparkling water of the Pacific Ocean on that older color television.

Jenna curled up on the bed when Sarah got there, having finished a phone call with her friend Barbara. Jenna wore her bathrobe over her pajamas, her body curled around what looked to be her pillow from her bed (Sarah could tell because it looked like the purple polka dot pattern of Jenna's sheets), and the blanket their mother left on the bed for them to use when they watched television resting on top of her.

Sarah wasn't hot. In fact, her feet felt a little warm in her winter slippers. When she stretched out on the bed, she let them slip off her feet and heard the thud as they hit the floor.

"Are you sick?" she asked Jenna who only shook her head. "What's wrong then?"

"Tired," Jenna mumbled.

"Then you must be tired and cold?" Sarah asked.

"No, not cold."

"But you're wrapped up like you are." Sarah reached over to pull the bathrobe off her sister, but Jenna pulled it right back toward her.

"Leave me alone."

Sarah gave up. She looked at Jenna about a minute longer then shrugged her shoulders. It was Jenna's choice. It didn't bother her so much that she was acting weird as Sarah knew her sister better than anyone else. But this weirdness wasn't like her.

*****

Their relationship, as they had called it, with baseball changed over the years. Evolved, was the word Sarah preferred to use. She liked to think they understood more of the game itself. The thought often made her laugh. The older they got, the more fanatic they became although they had never gone to one of "those" Cubs conventions. They thought they were a little silly and preferred to keep their love for the sport out of such a fan arena.

"A bunch of old guys who can't let go of their baseball dreams," Sarah would snort and Jenna would laugh.

"We just like their forearms," Jenna then would add about the players.

Yes, it was about the forearms from the point they discovered boys. It was Sarah first but Jenna followed close behind.

"We should rate them," Sarah suggested one fall day when they watched the division series championship on Columbus Day, grateful for the day off to watch baseball. It wasn't about sleeping in, it was about watching the Mets and the Dodgers duke it out for a chance to play in the World Series.

"That's a great idea," Jenna had cried. They laid on their parents' bed, watching on the television there. Jenna ran to her room and got a notebook and pen. When she returned she flew onto the bed, almost hitting their sleeping Sharpei, Nellie. (Named after Nellie, the annoying girl who always taunted Laura in "The Little House on the Prairie." Their mother insisted it was an awful name for a dog but it had stuck and they still loved her).

"Let's do it on a scale of one to ten because that will be easy," Sarah said, knowing Jenna would follow her "older sister's" knowledge on this one.

Sarah loved to remember those moments of her life with Jenna. She wondered if Jenna would remember them the same way she did. However, she could picture her sister saying, "I never flew across the bed and hit Nellie!" Sarah always thought that if she wrote a book about their life together and Jenna got a chance to read it, she would hand it back to Sarah filled with red marks. Her corrections of what *really* happened.

*****

As promised, on that first Sunday afternoon in March, Mark Lennon drove up to Sarah's house to pick up the cookies. Mairzy growled and Sarah stopped to talk with him while he walked up the flagstone path. "Don't embarrass me," she whispered, as if it made a difference and Mark could hear what she was saying from outside. "Act like a normal dog, please. I'll give you one of those rawhide bones that you like so much if you just act like a normal dog."

Mairzy didn't listen, growling and barking as Sarah pulled open the front door. "Hi," she called over Mairzy. "It'll just take a minute. He's pretty protective of me."

When Mairzy quieted down and Mark had walked through the door, Sarah led him to the kitchen where she had the cookies packaged in large catering dishes.

"Do you live here alone?" he asked looking around.

"With Mairzy," she pointed.

Mark looked surprised. "What?" Sarah asked him. "Did you think I was a lesbian?

He laughed. "No, I thought you were married with a couple of kids. The only people I've ever known to make cookies that good are moms."

"These are far from mom cookies," Sarah said. "They are teen girl cookies perfected."

"What do you mean?" he asked, looking into the dishes at the stacks of round desserts. "These are absolutely perfect. What are teen girl cookies though?"

Sarah blurted it out before she could stop herself. "My sister and I used to make these cookies."

"Did she help you make these?" He pointed at the aluminum dishes.

"No," Sarah stammered realizing it had been a long time since she mentioned her sister to anyone. A long time since she had to be vague enough about it to avoid further questions.

"Then she must not live here?" he asked. "Can I try one?"

Sarah shrugged her shoulders, using her refrigerator to hold her up. "They're yours. Or at least they are once you pay me for them."

Mark held up a finger. "You have a point there." He reached into his pocket and pulled out a check.

"Thank you," Sarah said.

"Oh, my, are these great!" he said, devouring one and stopping himself from eating two.

As she helped him carry the cookies to his truck, he stopped at the table near the front door. A large folder for the Northwestern University graduate programs rested on top of several books she promised to give to her friend Mandy.

"Are you going back to school?" Mark asked, stopping in front of the colorful folder topped with happy people. His hands filled with cookies, he tilted his head toward it. She noticed he had the softest brown eyes. Sarah was afraid if she started to talk, it all might tumble from her like a glass filled with water when it was knocked over.

"I'm thinking about getting my doctorate."

"Very cool," he said, opening the front door. And she was glad that was all he asked. She still wasn't ready to share her dream with anyone.

CHAPTER 8

There is a darkness that can suck the hope out of a person. A darkness that doesn't end. The one that Huey Lewis sings about in his song "Walking on a Thin Line" about Vietnam veterans. After Jenna died, Sarah found herself waking up in the middle of the night in the pitch black of her apartment, the only sound coming from the creaking of the building shifting and the refrigerator switching on and off.

At first, it was like life was normal. As it always had been. If she couldn't get back to sleep right away, she'd think about school, about the paper she had to write, the upcoming test. Then she would be reminded that Jenna was gone. Sarah would count the days since she died. First it was two weeks, then a month, then two months. It felt like she woke up at least once a week like this.

As she lay there, thinking about Jenna and missing her, still processing that her sister was no longer alive, she'd also think about her future. What would she do without Jenna? Their lives had been intertwined as if they had been woven together. Despite their differences, the many that they had, they still had the one common goal of the bakery. And they had baseball.

It didn't feel safe in the dark. It made Sarah nervous. Maybe she'd always been that way but hadn't realized it. That wasn't true. She remembered when she and Jenna and her friend Kelly would sleep outside on the deck in the summer, each one of them in a lounge chair, thinking they were cool because they were outside surrounded by lightning bugs. One night, around 11:00, late for them, they went into the front yard and saw a car coming down the road. "Duck like rocks!" Sarah had whispered and they each huddled into the sleeping bags that they walked around in. It was silly now, but it was the sort of fun memory that Sarah wished Jenna were still around, to remind her that darkness hadn't been all bad.

Now it represented a long day that would not end. A long night that felt endless. There isn't hope in darkness. She had begun to read about suicide and the despair that people who are suicidal feel. She wished she could put her finger on what it was that caused her sister to end her life. At least then she could attach something to it, make it feel better in some way. That probably would never happen though, she knew. Instead, she lay in bed, the moon half full and not giving out much light, wishing that dawn would come. Not that she wanted to start a new day but at least then she could feel more hopeful than she felt now. And less alone.

*****

Sarah often joked that Mairzy was the man in her life. "You don't look like the kind of person to have a German Shepherd," people sometimes said. Sarah would laugh and wonder exactly what that meant. Was she supposed to be some big, bad bully to have a GSD? She didn't care though, patting Mairzy's head as they walked away from the other person and their commentary.

Just as Sarah thought she might have been married with kids by the time she hit thirty, in hindsight a dog was something she never thought she would have. The family dog, Nellie, died a year before Jenna and although Jenna begged for a new dog, their parents reminded her that she, too, would be leaving home.

"You can get a dog when you get out of college," they repeated, much to her annoyance. Sarah sympathized with her sister. She and Matt had spent their entire lives surrounded by dogs. Their parents got a dog when Matt was just three and they weren't without one until Nellie died.

Getting a dog wasn't on Sarah's list though. She had enough to do without taking care of anyone. But she didn't tell anyone that the thought of taking care of anything scared her. She kept thinking that if she couldn't help keep her sister in the world, how could she think she could be a good parent, or even a good dog parent.

That first year of teaching and coaching, Sarah wasn't sure which way was up. If she wasn't teaching, she was running off to coach her first girls' tennis team. And if she wasn't coaching, she had papers to grade.

The girls walked off the courts late one September afternoon, Indian Summer apparent after the first cold spell of the fall. Sarah followed the girls, leaving her last to lock the gate. As she checked it she heard, "Ohhhhh" and "Ahhhhh" coming from them. They all gathered around something. When Sarah got closer, she saw it as black and it was moving. A puppy. A puppy with large black ears sticking out of its head.

"Oh how cute," the girls cooed. The dog wagged its tail. One of the girls dumped water of out her jug into a cup and slid it under the dog's tongue.

"What is it?" Someone asked and yet another one looked under the tail.

"It's a boy."

"What will we do with him?"

Sarah stood and watched. She was supposed to be the adult and her first thought was that she had to figure out how to act like the adult. What did she do? The dog didn't have a collar. There were no tags. What would they do with a dog?

"Coach, what do we do?" one of the girls asked and suddenly ten sets of eyes stared at her waiting for an answer. An answer they planned to act on.

She shook her head. "Well, does anyone need a dog?" she asked hopefully. The girls looked at each other and shook their heads.

"We already have two," one girl said.

"My mom is allergic to dogs, or at least that's what she tells us," another said.

After each of them had an excuse, Sarah knew that meant the dog, who also looked at her, was to go home to her apartment. The very place she didn't think she was allowed to have pets. Or at least she didn't know. "Okay, I'll take the dog home," she relented. The girls all cheered and someone picked him up and took him to Sarah's car.

"Maybe Coach won't be a good dog guardian though," one of the girls realized. They all appeared to have second thoughts.

"Wait," Sarah said, pulling her head out of the backseat of her car, where she cleared space for the dog from among the tennis rackets. "Why do you think that?"

The girls looked at each other. The one who held the dog seemed as if her arms were getting tired. "Can we just make a decision?" The dog began to squirm, wanting to be let down.

"Don't let go of the dog," someone else said. "He might run away."

"Then put him in Coach's car," another cried. "We're going to have to trust that Coach can handle him."

When people came over and met Mairzy, that was the story she told. She inherited the dog from her first tennis team, a group of girls who didn't believe she could care for a dog. But she did it because they challenged her. Little did they know, the challenge was a greater one for her than she anticipated.

That night, she and Mairzy stared at each other. "Well, now what do we do?" she asked the still-unnamed dog. "You'd think I'd be better at this than I am. I've been around dogs all my life. Maybe I'm afraid of attaching myself to anything."

Mairzy had made himself at home, already peeing in the hallway when he checked out the apartment. "You don't come trained," Sarah reminded herself out loud. She picked up Mairzy and placed him on the couch next to her. Mairzy looked as if he was listening to Sarah, although probably not understanding a word. Sarah quit talking and let her head fall back onto the couch. Thinking about how much she wished she could go to sleep and forget everything that she needed to do for the next day, she felt Mairzy reach toward her and rest his nose on her tennis skirt.

Sarah opened her eyes and stared at Mairzy who looked up. "Well, I guess if you need a home, then there probably is not a much better place than with me." Mairzy snuggled closer and Sarah rested her left hand on Mairzy's stomach. "Somehow we'll become a family," she told the dog. "Somehow."

She named Mairzy the next morning when she turned the dial on the radio, looking for her usual morning station, and she heard a song her dad often sang when he washed the dishes, "Mairzy Doats."

"That's your name," Sarah said, hoping Mairzy would agree. He peed on the kitchen floor.

*****

Thursday at lunch, Sarah worked on her laptop in her classroom looking up information on the Internet. The Northwestern folder was with her on this day. She had to get the application finished and sent to the graduate school. There was no more delaying it. If she wanted admission into the fall program, it had to be finished. She used every excuse in the world to not do it including cleaning the house's windows and screens, inside and outside. At least that time gave her an idea of something to write about for her essay. Now if she could sit down long enough to actually write the essay.

"Hey!" Mark poked his head into her classroom doorway again. She was getting used to seeing the top half of his body. "We sold all your cookies!" He walked in and made himself at home. Sarah knew then that the essay wasn't going to get finished. She dropped her hands off the laptop keyboard and decided she'd let him talk.

"That's great, I'm glad to hear it."

She hadn't noticed that he had one hand behind his back and as he pulled it to where she could see, a t-shirt came into view. "I brought you one of the t-shirts. You really are the biggest booster this year with what you've done for us."

"Happy to," Sarah said, taking the baseball t-shirt. Part of her wanted to giggle. Jenna would have loved it.

Once again he seated himself on a desk. "I still don't know why you don't sell your cookies," he said. "Why don't you have a cookie business?"

Oooh, Sarah thought, he's treading in deep water. How can I get him to stop? She quickly looked at the clock ticking away on the wall. There were still thirty minutes left in the lunch period. That wouldn't help. The kids wouldn't come in until ten minutes before the lunch bell. She wished she had to go to the bathroom. Something, anything.

"Um, let's say it just didn't work out."

"Why not?" He wasn't going to let up.

"I majored in nutrition and business in my undergrad."

"Then why are you teaching English?"

"I have my master's degree in education, specifically teaching English."

He didn't move, she didn't move. She felt like an interviewee who lost control of the interview.

Finally, she just didn't answer. The pause was long. He was patient though. He was a baseball coach, she remembered. Jenna would sit by her saying,

"Duh, if he can sit through all those games, he probably goes to church every Sunday morning, too."

"Why do you want to know?" she finally asked. She had the right to ask that question, didn't she?

"I'm trying to understand how a woman as pretty as you isn't married, makes great cookies, and is thinking about getting a doctorate. Don't you have a boyfriend? I don't think you're a lesbian."

Sarah thanked herself for not taking a drink of water. She thought she might have spit it out. She shrugged her shoulders. "If I had any say in it, my life would have been totally different. But you know the saying, that one about the best laid plans going awry?" And then she couldn't stop herself. The waterfall had begun. She wanted to clap her hand over her mouth but her hands sat in her lap folded together. "There was a reason I have a bachelors degree in nutrition and business."

"You were going to have your own nutritional consultant business? There's lots of work there. People always need help with the way they eat."

"No, that wasn't it. A cookie business. A bakery. Maybe a coffee shop and bakery."

The clock ticked. Five minutes and Mike Pearson would walk into the room and tell her about the girl he had tried to ask out that day.

"What happened? Why didn't you do it?" He looked around the room almost in disgust as if she had failed. "Why are you here?"

Fine, he wasn't going away. Maybe this would make him go away. "My sister, the one who I made the cookies with?" He nodded. "She killed herself her senior year in high school. We were going to do it together."

Mark slowly nodded his head. Mike Pearson walked in the room and broke the heavy air. It was as if he had a steak knife with him.

"Hey, Ms. McCall." Sarah waved at him. "I'll be with you in a minute, Mike." She was never so thankful to see the socially awkward seventeen-year-old before.

"I'm sorry," Mark said.

Sarah shrugged her shoulders. What else could she do? Would she do? She smiled. "It's ten years of my life. You make the best of it and you go on. You become a teacher and try to catch the hopelessness that was missed in Jenna."

The kids filtered in now. "I need to go," Mark said. He looked uncomfortable. It wasn't Jenna's death though, she thought. It was the kids. She could sense he wanted to be alone with her and ask more questions. He had a class to teach. And she had to get her head back into the kids.

The kids began to flock to her desk and Mark disappeared as quickly as he had popped his head into her room.

Driving home in the rain, Sarah couldn't stop thinking about her conversation with Mark earlier that day. She'd had to shove it aside like a stack of papers to teach those final three classes in the afternoon, but it was Friday and now she could process it. Not that she thought about it that way. She wasn't sure what she thought where she would be at this point her life. But had she ever thought this far ahead?

With Jenna she had. Of course. They had plans to open the bakery. To make their cookies household names. But had they thought beyond that?

"I think we should buy ownership in a baseball team," Jenna said. "Then we'll have the pick of players to date."

Sarah rolled her eyes at her sister. "Like the owners should be dating the players," she reminded her. She knew sometimes there was a world of difference in their maturity levels. She always thought it was because Jenna was more creative. Sometimes Sarah teased Jenna she was out of touch with reality.

For so long she thought she was doing well. Her life was not what she thought it would be but she was still young enough that she had choices. Maybe she would still get married and have a family. Maybe she felt like she could go that route now. She knew it was different for her brother, Matt. He was married already when Jenna died. He and Donna had Chris just three years after Jenna died. She could still remember how happy her parents were, how Chris's birth took some of the sadness away.

But it wasn't that way for Sarah. After all, Matt was five years older than her, there were eight years between Matt and Jenna. He never felt very close to Sarah. While she'd never asked him, she didn't have to. His life was pretty well set when Jenna died. He had a great job; she was in college and all her post-college plans involved Jenna. When Jenna died, she had no idea what she was going to do. The bakery seemed silly without Jenna there to urge her on. And somehow her parents had found out about their plans after Jenna died.

"I don't know why you don't do it," Arlene McCall had said to Sarah that Christmas, the first one without Jenna, as she checked the turkey in the oven. "You're already almost done with college."

And that's when Sarah told them. Right there in the kitchen with snow falling outside and Matt and Donna pulling into the driveway. "I'm going to graduate school. I'm going to become a teacher."

She knew it wasn't that they were disappointed. She didn't disappoint her parents. How could they be? At least she kept forging forward even with her sister gone. They were too busy lost in their own grief anyway. It was only another semester. She could finish this one degree and then move on.

"Are you sure that's what you want to do?" her father asked, his eyes looking sad, just like she was sure they all looked on that day. The hair left on top of his head had thinned more in the past eleven months than she ever remembered in such a short period of time.

Sarah nodded her head. She didn't know what else to do. She knew she had to do something.

"We'll support you in whatever you do," he had said simply, walking to the door where Matt and Donna struggled to bring in several bags of wrapped gifts.

Had it been a mistake? Maybe all of it had been a mistake? So much happened in the ensuing years.

When Sarah got home, Mairzy waited for her. There was no spring tennis today with the weather. She gathered the girls a few times a week for strength training and sometimes a match or two. It was an early afternoon home for her and she sank into the couch and waited for darkness when she'd head over to Barbara's house to spend Friday night with her best friend and their kids. At least she knew that would jolt her out of the funk Mark had put her in. No, that wasn't true. She didn't want to fault him. He didn't know anything about her. She'd learned long ago not to judge people on their reactions to Jenna's death.

~ Sisters: The Karma Twist ~

Later that evening as she sat at Barbara's dining room table, the kids downstairs watching a movie, Barbara swirled her glass of white wine. "There's nothing like Friday night," she sighed, sitting back in her chair and raising her glass to make a toast. "The girls might have gymnastics tomorrow but at least I don't have to go to work. Yahoo to that."

Sarah raised her own glass and smiled. After she took a drink, she set it down and basked in the warmth of the brown walls and the chandelier that lit up the room. Even though the table was filled with dirty dishes, slowly leaving the room via Barbara's husband Jeff, it felt lived in. It was alive. Mairzy, who'd made the trip to see the kids, lay at her feet snoozing, having been climbed all over for an hour before dinner. Looking around, Sarah spoke, "Are you content, Barbara?"

Barbara's eyes were shut, her hair falling off the back of her head from where she attempted to get as horizontal as she could, resting her feet on the chair across the underside of the table from her. "Mmmmm, at the moment? Yes, I am."

"No, with your life."

Barbara's eyes popped open. "Well, I am now but I might change my mind by the time I have to put the munchkins to bed." She sat back up at the table, trying to reorient herself to the real world by looking around. Sarah thought she sought the answers from the walls of her house around her and the dirty pizza dishes on the table. "Yes, I am. I think we always doubt ourselves and the decisions we've made but overall I'm glad I'm here. I'm glad I have Jeff and the girls. And even though I complain about it, I love teaching."

Sarah nodded her head. She could see Barbara turning her attention away from herself. "You're doubting it all, aren't you?"

Sarah nodded, leaning forward. "I haven't in a long time."

"But it was ten years two weeks ago. It makes sense."

She and Barbara had been friends in high school. They played on the tennis team together although Sarah had been the better of the two. Barbara didn't care. She had a good time. Sarah still missed the whack of the tennis balls when they played and talked about boys. Whatever she couldn't discuss with Jenna, she knew she could talk about with Barbara. Barbara had stuck with her after Jenna died, even though they attended college several states away from each other. Barbara often joked that she had to take a part-time job just to pay for the calls she made to check on Sarah where Sarah would cry for an hour.

"You wish you had a family?" Barbara asked. Sarah loved her friend for supporting her as she became a teacher and coach, even attending as many tennis matches as she could, her bored kids in tow.

Sarah shrugged her shoulders. "We're only in our early thirties. There's still time. But maybe there's not. I don't know." She paused as Jeff walked in to take more dishes.

"Don't let me interrupt your conversation," he said.

"We won't, honey, don't worry," Barbara said, pouring herself more wine.

"I got asked to make some cookies for a fundraiser," Sarah admitted, proceeding to tell what happened with Mark.

"Oh." Barbara was quiet. Sarah knew she was thinking but what she said instead surprised her. "The tarot cards." Sarah shook her head, letting her friend know she couldn't go there.

CHAPTER 9

Sarah spent at least a half hour with Mairzy each evening. No matter how tired she was, no matter how long the list of things she needed to accomplish before going to bed and returning to school the next morning, she and Mairzy sat on the couch together. Sometimes Sarah talked to Mairzy, other times they sat silently. And yet other times they watched television.

"Thanks for being such a good friend," Sarah would whisper while Mairzy snoozed happily.

That holiday season, the first when she was teaching, the first when she had Mairzy, and the first without her parents, Sarah was especially grateful for the dog. Her small Christmas tree, given to her by her mother when they moved to Florida ("I don't ever plan to decorate for Christmas again," her mother lamented both because Jenna was gone and because she was moving to Florida with no intention to return to the Chicago area) stood in a corner looking lonely. Sarah wasn't used to pathetic looking Christmas trees. She'd been raised on big holiday seasons. Now she spent them with Matt and his family, always feeling like an outsider among Donna's family. Sometimes she wished she was home with Mairzy. At least then she felt like she was with family.

"We heard your team made it to state," Donna's father, the only one interested in talking to her, would ask at the dinner table. "I saw it in the newspaper and pointed it out to Ellen that it was your team."

Dinner would be the only time the conversation would revolve around Sarah. Not that she expected it to but sometimes it was nice to be acknowledged. Most of all, she missed the acknowledgement of Jenna as their sister. As part of their family. During the family prayer, Matt leading since it was his house, he always asked for blessings of family members not with them, but by "not with them," Matt meant those still living. He never mentioned Jenna there either.

Thanksgiving. Christmas Eve. Christmas Day. They all became one in the same. Torture.

"We're having such a great time," her mother would say on the phone from Florida and Sarah would wonder if she meant it. At first she understood their need not to come home for the holidays. They wanted a change. They finished raising kids. They had a sense of failure that they hadn't completed the job since Jenna didn't make it to her high school graduation. It was easier to run away. And she understood, especially on the snowiest mornings when she was outside grumbling about having to shovel the driveway before she left for work, why they didn't want to shovel snow anymore.

But Sarah didn't understand how they couldn't come back. Time had passed. There were grandchildren. Yet she was too afraid to ask. So she didn't.

Each Thanksgiving and Christmas morning for the first five years after Jenna died, Sarah drove to the cemetery before going to her brother's house, to see her sister's grave. She had to remember to bring a broom with her if there was snow. Or to tread carefully through the mud after a storm. One year it sleeted as she stood out there, alone, among the graves. Among the people who had passed on to another life.

She knew she shouldn't feel alone in a cemetery. It wasn't meant to be a lonely place despite how horror movies portrayed it. It was filled with past lives and the stories that went with those lives. But Sarah also knew she probably thought differently about cemeteries before her sister died. They only went once a year to put flowers on the graves of family members she'd never met before. Now her sister was there. Although she didn't visit often, since her parents had moved and she knew her brother didn't visit, she felt it was up to her to go and pay a "visit" to Jenna. It wasn't about respect. It was to visit her sister.

Once she moved up north, to the northern suburbs, where she bought a house closer to the school where she taught, Sarah only returned to Cedarville about once a year when she visited Julie's family. Slowly, the past continued to slip through her hands. She tried to grab some of it but it was too much for her to handle on her own. No one else wanted to help and she found it was time to let it go.

There was a glimmer of light for her though in her Aunt Esther and Uncle Don. They invited Sarah over every few months for dinner on a Saturday or Sunday evening. "Just let us know what works best for you," Aunt Esther, would call out in her sing-song voice on the phone. Sarah always felt she would break out into song like in a musical, disappointed when she didn't.

Esther was her father's sister and they were the only other family that lived nearby since all her grandparents had died or moved before her parents moved to Florida. Sarah loved to visit their split-level house, still stuck in the early 1980s, the last time they remodeled it. Each time she went to see them, they told her about their latest happening like getting their wood floors redone. It always was a drama with them. They didn't have anything else to talk about though so she let them share the details of their pain-in-the-ass contractor.

"We're so glad to see you!" they would exclaim each time she came through the door. It was the fulfillment she wasn't getting from her own family although Esther and Don had been Jenna's Godparents. She loved leaving their house with a large brown paper shopping bag filled with Tupperware containers of food. Sometimes it was the leftovers from the dinner they had eaten that night, other times Esther filled them with cookies. She was constantly in motion, constantly cooking and baking, as she always had.

And since her son, Sarah's cousin, Gary had moved to Colorado, she had no one to dote on. Instead she doted on Sarah who was glad to have the attention. Sarah just wished she could visit more often. She didn't see them on holidays because they went to visit Gary.

"I miss Jenna," Sarah said to them one night, about four years after Jenna died.

Esther and Don looked at each other, each putting their fried chicken down. "We've been wanting to ask you, "Esther said quietly, "but we were afraid it might upset you."

Sarah shook her head. "Everyone is so afraid to talk about it. I don't get it. I want to talk about her. I want to talk about her life. But it's like because she ended it, ended it on a way none of us agree with, no will talk about her now."

"Oh dear, we're happy to remember your sister," Esther said, getting up from the table and washing her hands. The dishtowel still in her hand drying them, she walked out of the room, returning with a stack of photos. "Keep eating. We'll look at these after we're done. I've been saving them for you," she said, placing them in the middle of the table.

The top photo was one of Sarah and Jenna at Christmas when Jenna was two. Sarah began to cry. Why didn't anyone else get this?

*****

Sarah struggled to feel her sister's presence with her. In the weeks after Jenna's death, she began to look for books that would help her to understand not only what this grief road was about, but also this "suicide survivor" thing she kept reading that she was now a part of. She didn't get it at all. "Survivors are people who escape plane crashes," she told her roommate Celia with a book in her hand simply called *Suicide Survivors*.

Celia always listened patiently. What could she say? Sarah didn't expect her to say or do anything. She realized she had no expectations for anyone. Including herself. This was much too confusing. She wished she had a map, something at least to guide her and let her know what was ahead. Was that so much to ask for?

*****

Jenna's room was filled with life. Jenna's life. And Jenna's love of life. Or so everyone, Sarah included, always had thought. When Sarah returned home after the end of school, a few months after her sister's death, the door to Jenna's room was shut. She knew it was because her mother couldn't bear to walk by every day, on her way to the linen closet, on her way to the office (once Matt's bedroom), and see that Jenna was no longer there. Sarah knew her mother walked into Jenna's room sometimes and would begin talking to her before stopping mid-sentence, realizing she was dead. And she still probably saw Jenna's lifeless body each time she walked into her room. Sarah knew this because she heard it happen several times in the first days that she was home from college. Finally, her mother shut the door and kept it shut.

Sarah was alone in the house when she chose to open the door, fully realizing her sister wasn't there. The sun bounced off the lavender walls as it always did. Jenna's bed was made, probably because their mother couldn't stand the sight of it unmade. Maybe it confused her that Jenna was just down the hall in the bathroom. Or maybe it made her feel better to make it. Sarah sat on the bed at first looking around and taking in the surroundings of a life that she had known since she was three years old and their parents brought her home from the hospital. A life she now shook her head wondering about, how Jenna's love for life could be lost, ending long before it really began.

Sarah stood up and walked to Jenna's desk, her books piled on top along with a half-finished math assignment. She left in the midst of life, Sarah thought, picking up the trigonometry assignment and sliding her finger next to the pencil that lay beside to it. What had really happened? Had Jenna snapped in the midst of homework and decided life was too hard? That wasn't Jenna. For as many times as they had discussed the difficulties of life, surely Jenna would have called her. And it certainly couldn't have been over trigonometry.

None of it made sense. She always called Sarah when she was upset about something or tried to work through something. Why wouldn't she call her this time? Sarah sat at the wood desk, one that came from her maternal grandparents house when they moved to Arizona, and opened the top right drawer. At first she hesitated. These were her sister's things. Sarah never went through them and vice versa. At least since they'd been out of junior high when Jenna's jealousy toward Sarah reached an all-time high and she tore through some things in Sarah's room. But Sarah didn't want to think about that on this day. She needed to find clues, reasons, an explanation why her sister ended her life.

In the top right drawer, Sarah found what she realized were Jenna's journals. The very journals she didn't know that her sister kept. She always said she didn't have time for something like that. She didn't want to reflect on the past when she could look forward to the future.

Several wirebound notebooks, usually leftover from classes, filled with thoughts, writings, and, sometimes, daily events. Sarah took them out of the drawer and placed them on the desk in front of her, carefully, because she hoped they held the clues she needed.

There wasn't much to read at first. Lots of made up poems about crushes. A few bakery ideas, all of which Sarah knew about, and then getting halfway through the first one, the mood began to change. There were no dates but there were paragraphs, some in different colors of ink as if she had written them at different times, of pain and sadness.

A fear developed in the entries. "I don't know what's wrong with me" or "I can't stop the sadness." Sarah couldn't read much more. She closed the journal and set it on top of Jenna's desk. She had been right. Jenna was sick. And she had been afraid for anyone to find out.

That was all Sarah needed to know. A tear fell from her face and she sat on her sister's bed, holding one of the purple pillows close to her. "Why didn't you let me help you?" she cried. "I thought that's what we did for each other."

*****

Mark Lennon always mysteriously appeared in the doorway of Sarah's classroom when she worked at her desk. She was never standing at her white board or anywhere else in the room. Always at her desk.

This day she jumped when he said, "Hi."

"I'm sorry," he said, once again plopping his large frame onto one of the desks in the front row. "I didn't mean to scare you." She wasn't so sure by the smile on his face though. "I wanted to know if you could make more cookies. Apparently there was quite the word of mouth about them and we have people asking for them." Sarah started to open her mouth. She didn't want to do it. She didn't want to get in the regular habit of baking. Mark held out his arm to stop her. "I'm going to give you a bigger cut of the pie. I think we can sell these at every game."

Again, Sarah tried to stop it. And, again, he held out his arm. "I know you aren't coaching in the spring. Girls tennis is in the fall. You have the time to do this."

"But I don't want to," she said, startling herself at how quietly she said it.

"You don't want to? Why?" he asked. She realized he wasn't going to let her say no. Sarah looked down at her desk, feeling embarrassed. She didn't like being put in spots she didn't want to be. And who was Mark Lennon to make her feel this way? She felt like she should sit in one of the desks in her classroom, a sixteen-year-old girl feeling insecure. And not sure how to answer.

"You don't have a reason not to," Mark said, leaning forward. Sarah lifted her head toward him. "That's why you can't answer. And I won't take your sister's death as an excuse." She knew he'd trapped her and she sat back in her desk. Now she tried not to cry. That would be more embarrassing than not knowing what to say.

"I was thinking six dozen by Sunday. That gives you the weekend to do them."

Sarah nodded, looking out the window, looking beyond where Mark was sitting on the desk. "Okay."

He smiled and got up off the desk. "I'll let you get back to your grading," he said and turned to leave. But before he did, he turned back to her and asked, "Can I ask you a question?"

Sarah looked up at him, squishing her nose, figuring it was about Jenna but wishing it was about calorie content in the cookies.

"Is it true that you've turned down repeated dates from teachers here?"

Sarah didn't answer. She felt her eyes flash open. "Who told you that?"

He shrugged, that funny smile, the same one he showed when he told her he didn't mean to scare her, appeared on his face. "I heard a rumor."

Sarah tried not to look like she was concerned. After he left, she attempted to work. She tried to wrap her head back around the essay test she was writing. Mark Lennon had left her too much to ponder though. She shut everything down, shut off the lights, and drove home.

While she grated cheese for her spaghetti, she reached into her mental archive, the one she had felt surrounding her lately. It was as if her dining room table was filled with filing boxes of memories and Sarah sifted through them daily. This ten-year thing wasn't going away despite the anniversary of Jenna's death now six weeks past.

That night she thought about Ken again, her graduate school boyfriend. But it was different. She thought about the happy times. There had been a lot of them. She tried to cling to them and the times he made her laugh, the very reason she had begun to date him. The same reason she could let go of Jenna's death long enough to allow him into her life. He made her feel good. He made her feel like life could be okay.

Why couldn't she let anyone do that now? She wondered. Did Mark want to ask her out? Why didn't he just do it? No, she realized, he wasn't going to because he knew she'd turn him down.

It would be much easier if she could forget all the bad stuff, if she could focus on the happy memories. All the happy memories with Jenna. All the happy memories with her family. All the happy memories with Ken.

But somehow life didn't work that way. The imaginary boxes on her dining room table held *all* the memories: good, bad, and otherwise. And for some reason she had to spend time going through all of them, reaching into each box not knowing what was there, and examining each memory, each file, that she took out.

And after she spent time with each one, she could decide if she needed to keep it or not. Some she wanted to keep because they were happy memories with Jenna, ones she knew she wouldn't get back because Jenna had taken the other half of the memory with her. And others she knew might give her strength on the journey. She put those in a separate place, somewhere that she knew she could find them when she needed them.

Her favorite with Ken was the first of her two birthdays that she spent with him. He took her to see the Kansas City Royals play. The night before her birthday, although he had told her he had a surprise and not for her to plan anything for that day, he handed her an envelope. "I don't think it would be a good idea to surprise you with this tomorrow," he said, looking a little sheepish.

Sarah, who never cried during movies and couldn't understand why everyone else did, now cried openly when she saw what was inside. It wasn't the baseball tickets that made her cry. It was the thought behind the tickets. He had understood she didn't want that kind of surprise.

"You don't have to cry," he said. She felt his hand around her waist as he pulled her close. "I really wanted to do this for you." She felt his voice on her head as he spoke. "I didn't want to upset you though."

Sarah took a deep breath, her hands shaking. She pulled away so she could look at him, to see his blue eyes that she loved. "No, it's not that," she said, sniffling. "It's the thought. It's that you thought to give these to me the day before rather than surprising me tomorrow. Thank you."

When Sarah remembered that moment, and it wasn't often she replayed it in her head, she knew she had been wrong to give up something so great. She was scared though. She was scared he would leave her just as Jenna had.

CHAPTER 10

Mark appeared at 2:00 pm on the dot that Sunday for the cookies. And Sarah had them ready as she reluctantly told him she would.

"You have a talent, you know," he said, looking them over.

"My sister was the real baker," she said shrugging her shoulders. "She had the creative gene. I'm more the business nutrition girl."

"I still don't know why you're teaching in that crazy place when you could be making people happy by baking cookies."

"Nah," she said. "It's a lot of work for one person to do. Teaching is easier when you come down to it."

"On a bad day though? On a bad day when I want to bop the monsters in the head or my boys aren't listening out on the field, I'll take baking cookies. Even if it's a pay cut."

"But then you wouldn't have the sense of satisfaction the day the light bulb pops up over their heads that they actually understand something. Or they come from behind to win the game." She leaned on the counter by the sink, her arms behind her. She bounced back and forth, catching herself when she thought it might make her look nervous.

"Is that what keeps you teaching?"

Sarah nodded. "Essentially. At least I know somewhere down the line each student or athlete will remember something from me. And that's enough to keep me going. Even on a bad day."

"Maybe you should come to a game one day," Mark said. She thought he looked at her until she realized his eyes had moved past her to the refrigerator door.

"Where was that photo taken?" he asked, pointing.

Sarah turned. It was her with Jenna at Dodger Stadium, their favorite place outside of Wrigley Field. "We went to Los Angeles the summer before I went to college. My dad's brother lives there and took us."

"I take it you're a Cubs fan?" He pointed at the photo and the t-shirts she and Jenna wore.

"We were the minority, but we didn't care. We just loved being there. We always watched the late games here so for us it was great to be there and be part of what we knew was a late night here in Chicago."

She smiled at that memory although the rest of the trip hadn't been so happy. Something had been wrong with Jenna although Sarah couldn't pinpoint it at that time. She could see that Jenna was struggling to be her usual bubbly self. One night, Sarah woke up in the room they shared in their uncle's family's house and heard sniffling from the twin bed next to her.

"Are you okay? She asked Jenna turning around and hugging her own pillow.

"I'm fine," Jenna said. There was a defensiveness in her voice that Sarah didn't often hear. It usually only came out when she was asked to do something she didn't want to do. But she always had shared what was wrong. Why wouldn't she this time? "I have my period. I think it's making me emotional," she whispered, turning further away from Sarah, indicating the conversation had ended.

Sarah didn't go back to sleep right away. She thought about Jenna, about what was up, wishing she could do something to help her sister. But unless her sister reached back to her, it wasn't any use. Jenna held herself tightly. She didn't want to let Sarah in. Sarah didn't get it. She knew she could help her sister. She wanted to help her. She wished she could reach across the space between the beds and touch Jenna's shoulder to let her know she'd be okay. But something kept her arm under her pillow. It was as if a brick lay on top of it. She wasn't supposed to do it.

All those years since Jenna's suicide, she wondered why she was paralyzed. If she had forced the issue, maybe things would have been different. But as the years had gone on, she knew that wasn't true. It was more than one bad night. Something deep inside Jenna kept her from reaching out. Or accepting any of the help people tried to give her.

"What are you thinking about?" Mark asked.

~ Sisters: The Karma Twist ~

Sarah sighed and looked at him. "Nothing. Just that trip." She quickly changed the subject before he could ask anything. "How long do you think it'll take to sell these cookies?"

He shrugged, a confident shrug. "We have two games this week."

At that moment, Sarah realized she didn't want him to leave. She couldn't put her finger on it. She just didn't want him to go although he looked at his watch then. "I need to get back to my house," he said. "I've got papers to grade. Probably the same as you."

There was a shift that day. She wasn't sure what it was but she admitted to herself that she liked it. And when he began to show up in her classroom for a few minutes each day, at least to say hi, she told herself she liked that, too. She liked it so much that one day when she didn't see him, she strolled down the hall to his classroom and poked her head in where he was sitting at his desk looking just like her with his head down into a history test he was grading.

"Hey," she said. "I didn't see you."

She saw his face brighten when he saw her and she smiled back.

"I didn't realize I was obligated to daily visits with you," he said, jokingly.

"Yeah, me neither. But I need to go. I just wanted to make sure you weren't sick or anything."

And as quickly as Sarah had stopped, she turned around and walked to the front office, smiling all the way. At least that had been easy.

CHAPTER 11

Sarah wished she hadn't hated Jenna. Ever. Her mother often laughed about how unhappy Sarah had been when they brought Jenna home from the hospital. Soon Sarah was dragging her sister around the house just like one of her dolls although her mother said that she often treated her dolls better than Jenna. Jenna never seemed to mind any of these stories, instead using them as fuel against her sister when she wanted something. "Remember how you used to push me around in that baby stroller and then dump me out when you were done with me?" she reminded Sarah before asking if she could borrow something out of Jenna's closet. Sarah knew Jenna didn't remember any of that. Everyone else told her about it.

Sarah never felt like anyone quite understood what it was like for her in elementary school though. She wanted to be her own person. She didn't want her sister tagging along with her to the bus stop, to the church for CCD every Tuesday afternoon, around the neighborhood as she rode bikes with her friends. She wanted to be "Sarah," not "Sarah and Jenna." But Jenna didn't care. No matter how many times Sarah told her sister to go away, she kept coming right back just like one of those Weebles that they played with. They knocked them over, with their round bottoms, and they popped right back up. That was Jenna.

As the third anniversary of Jenna's death passed, Sarah remembered how she felt differently for the first time since Jenna died. She didn't feel as sad. Somewhere she remembered someone saying something about the "new normal" forming. Maybe, Sarah thought, by then she had accepted her new normal and that's why she felt that way at the three-year mark.

But at the three-year mark, she also couldn't let go of how mean she had been to Jenna. The thoughts always came back that maybe Jenna knew their time was short and refused to be derailed by Sarah's behavior. She couldn't explain it to Jenna though. Besides, Sarah knew she wouldn't get what Jenna was saying anyway. Sarah tried to imagine how a conversation like that might go.

"Don't be so mean to me," Jenna would have said, holding her arms out in front of her, palms facing Sarah, as if to stop her. "We only have a few more years left."

"What is that supposed to mean?" Sarah would have reacted, her hands on her hips. "You don't know that."

"But I do," Jenna would try to explain.

Sarah knew she never would have understood. They were supposed to grow old together as sisters. She hoped they weren't going to grow old together as the "spinster sisters" like their dad's distant cousins who had never married and lived together for the rest of their lives. Sarah just thought in some way they would be part of each other's lives as they had planned with the bakery.

Three years. Three dozen cookies. A new normal. And the year that Sarah started to coach girls tennis. The year they made state and everyone thought it was a fluke that a first year coach, one who looked much like her athletes, could accomplish such a feat.

"Next year we're going to win it," she would mumble under her breath after people walked up to her and said, "We thought you were one of the players, not the coach."

That summer, as she and the girls trained, running endless laps around the track and lifting weights in the school's weight room that never got lighter, she spent her evenings in her rented townhouse reading about sports psychology. It reminded her of the mental games she and Jenna played with each other during their own high school athletic careers.

"Duh! Whoever swims the fastest wins," Sarah would tease her sister to which Jenna would reply, "If you'd just hit the ball so hard they couldn't hit it back, you'd win, too. Duh!" And so the games would begin. They never actually trained together since Jenna spent most of her time in the pool and Sarah on the tennis courts.

There were a few times they ran together though, usually around spring break when they were bored and home alone, making grand plans for the summers they thought would be perfect if they had the perfect bodies. And after a winter of staying inside and eating butter-filled cookies, they were anxious to get out and be in the fresh air. They went out in their heavy sweatshirts and sweat pants, sweating up a storm on a mid-morning in March when the Midwestern weather showed its fickle side.

But what Sarah missed most were the signs they made for each other, encouraging each other, just as they did with their teammates, for invitationals, conferences, meets, and anything else that was important. Sometimes even on bad days.

And that's what she passed on to the girls she coached. That first year she implemented what would become traditions for them, sharing and connecting with each other. And the talks she gave them each ensuing year as she watched her teams develop and grow.

"You should have been a sports psychologist," Barbara often said to her, showing another article in the *Chicago Tribune* about Sarah's team.

"I don't think so," Sarah would laugh, pushing the article away. "I did more than my fair share of school."

"What? You *go* to high school each day," Barbara laughed back. "The joke's on you."

"I just heard you're known for your motivational techniques," Mark said, once again strolling into Sarah's classroom as if he worked there as well. She looked up, like she always did, and waited to hear what else he might have to say before she responded. But this time he sat on the usual desk, in his usual style, and looked at her.

"Um, yeah," she finally said, looking around as if a non-existent person in the room might help her.

"I want to hear about them," he said, leaning forward.

"Well, I'm not sure they would work for baseball," she said, pointing her pencil at him. "I coach girls. They're a little different to work with."

"Try me," he said. "You've had seven teams go to state and three of them place. Obviously you're doing something right."

"Girls need to learn to support each other and motivate each other," Sarah said. "It's pretty simple when you think about it. It's fostering a family. I just happen to be lucky that I have great girls."

"But you know something about technique, too."

"Sure, of course," she said, putting the pencil down. "But you can have all the technique in the world and still be a horrible team."

He laughed and they both looked when they heard the classroom door open and several students walked in. "True," Mark said, getting off the desk. "Some day I'll get you to tell me your secret though."

Sarah shook her head as he left.

By then, the secret had been out for some time though. Countless people listened to her speak about it and asked her about it. That was why she was continually asked to make more presentations about how she motivated her teams and built team unity. Now she got offers from other states thanks to the Internet spreading the word. Mark seemed to be the last to know though.

CHAPTER 12

"We're going to church," Arlene McCall said, putting on her wristwatch when Sarah walked into the kitchen on a Sunday morning the summer after Jenna's death.

"Okay," Sarah said simply, reaching for a mug to fill with coffee and read the *Chicago Tribune*. The day was not just sunny but also bright. Sarah's eyes adjusted for the light outside not realizing her mother was still behind her.

"Do you want to go?" her mother asked.

Sarah turned and shook her head. She could see the disappointment in her mother's eyes. "God and I aren't speaking," Sarah said simply, turning back to the coffee maker.

"That's more reason to go," her mother said, watching her father walk into the room. "You can't be angry at God forever about Jenna."

Tapping her fingers on the countertop, she turned back to her mother, "Then why would God allow this to happen? Why would this God that we're supposed to love and worship and let guide our lives let Jenna end hers?"

"Sarah, don't say that," her mother said, holding out her hand.

"Mom, I know the church means a lot to you but please let me be." Sarah turned her back again to her mother and took a drink of her coffee. Behind her, she knew her father ushered her mother to the car. And he shook his head to leave Sarah alone.

Sarah could look back after ten years and see that was the beginning of the end of her relationship with her parents as the relationship had been during what she began to call "The Jenna Years." Instead of church, she would walk into Jenna's room and sort through her sister's life. It was a project in itself, deciding what should be kept, what should be donated, who wanted what. Although it had sunk in that Jenna wasn't coming back,

Sarah still couldn't bring herself to being comfortable rifling through her sister's things. It was her life and the more time Sarah spent dismantling her room, the more reality began to set in that Jenna was definitely gone.

There wasn't even an easy place to start. Where did you start when someone died? Sarah wondered, standing in the middle of the room. There was no map for this. Just as there was no map for coping with suicide loss. Sarah wished someone would have handed her a manual and told her everything she would have to cope with and logistically take care of. Why wasn't that possible to do? She didn't think the grief journey of each person would be the same yet weren't there enough similarities that someone could create some sort of map? She remembered the books they had as kids, the ones where you had two choices at the end of each chapter and whichever one you chose took you to a different chapter and sometimes a different ending. Now that would be good.

She walked over to Jenna's closet and opened the doors. In front of her was everything that Jenna wore. Sarah couldn't take them down yet. At first she had to look at each item and remember them. They all looked familiar. The dresses from the school dances. The dresses from the family gatherings and events. The dress from Matt's wedding to Donna. She and Jenna had both been in the wedding, standing at the altar feeling silly in those puffy pink dresses. What was Donna thinking? They had laughed because it was the only way they could cope with having to wear something so awful.

"We'll get her back one day," Jenna had promised when they were standing in their parents' bedroom in front of their mother's full-length mirror.

"Get who back?" Their mother had asked, walking into the room in her mother-of-the-groom dress that at least wasn't so puffy.

"Donna," they said in unison.

"Oh girls," Arlene McCall said, clucking her tongue. "She's going to be your sister-in-law today. Be nice to her. Just because you two have such a close bond doesn't mean you need to force her out."

"Uh Mom," Sarah said, "It's not about that." She pointed at her dress. "Would you be happy wearing this?"

"It's what Donna picked," her mother reminded her, being the partial, kind person she always was.

Sarah and Jenna often plotted how they would get Donna back though. "By the time we get married she'll probably be done having kids so it won't be useful to make her wear anything that makes her look like an Easter egg," Jenna had sighed.

"You have to be sure we're going to get married one day," Sarah reminded her sister. "After all, she might be the one having the last laugh if we don't."

"Maybe you're convent bound but I'm not," Jenna had laughed. With her self-confidence seemingly failing some days in those last years, Sarah smiled, just glad that Jenna looked toward a future with someone. "You know, we could get married at Wrigley Field. Maybe we could marry baseball players."

Jenna the dreamer was alive and well that day, Sarah remembered. What amazed her was how many conversations she could recall as if they just happened. She would remember them laying on their parents bed or lounging outside in the backyard on the deck. No matter where they were, baseball always played on the television. Or the radio. Harry Caray and Steve Stone made up the background noise. The crack of a bat when it connected with the ball. That all made Sarah smile. Or they were in the kitchen messing with their oatmeal cookie recipe.

But what scared her were the things she couldn't remember. After Jenna died, she began to fear forgetting her. She left an old message on her answering machine just so she could play it sometimes and be reminded of Jenna's vivacious laugh. She pulled out her photo so she didn't forget her smile or her eyes that always sparkled. She had the means to remember these parts of Jenna. What she didn't have was access to all their conversations, to each time they talked about something, even the arguments about who used the hair gel last. Sarah knew Jenna took some of that with her. She wouldn't get it all back. That's what bothered her most.

She pulled the dresses out of the closet; she had black trash bags to fill with everything. "We'll donate most of it to the women's shelter," her mother suggested. "At least there are people there who can use her clothes and accessories." Sarah wondered if the women would need prom and homecoming dresses. When did women escaping from abusive husbands need this sort of thing? It didn't matter though. She was sure they would find some use for them. The dresses and the shoes gone, the closet looked bare. The swimsuits, a dozen of them that Jenna kept, even though several looked as though they were worn to threads, were thrown away. Her underwear, thrown away. Things you couldn't donate. Sarah took a few

T-shirts, particularly the Cubs ones, and donated the rest. Slowly the hall filled with bags while the room emptied out. Her parents had stayed at church for the monthly pancake breakfast and then usually met several other couples for coffee. The house stayed quiet for the rest of the morning.

Sarah heard their voices downstairs as she closed the last drawer of Jenna's dresser and sighed. The clothes and accessories were sorted. There was still the rest of her life to go but it felt as though the biggest chunk had been completed.

"Oh," was all her mother said when she turned the corner from the stairs into the hallway. "I didn't realize how much clothing she owned."

Sarah stood in the doorway of her sister's room. "Amazing, isn't it?"

The next day would be harder, dropping it off at the women's shelter, a task Sarah did by herself with her parents at work. It wasn't actually the shelter since that was undisclosed, but an office where donations could be taken. A nondescript little house just off the business district. Set on a corner, it was one of the last houses left, the rest torn down and turned into Taco Bells and Jiffy Lubes.

"I called about a big donation of clothing," Sarah told the woman at the desk when she walked inside. She wasn't prepared for their reaction as she began to bring the bags into the building though.

"We thought you meant a few bags," the two women said, looking at each other, "We didn't realize you meant this many."

Sarah just smiled. She had dropped off a life.

"Where did all of this come from?" one of the women asked, poking her hand into one of the bags and seeing what was inside.

"My sister died," Sarah said. "These were all hers."

"Oh," the shorter of the two women said. "I'm so sorry. We'll make sure they go to someone who can use them."

"What happened?" the taller woman asked.

Sarah took a deep breath. They asked. She would tell. "She killed herself a few months ago."

~ Sisters: The Karma Twist ~

Both women shook their heads and the shorter one spoke. "We see that sometimes here, sadly. Women think there is no way out. We'll make sure her clothes get a second life." She handed Sarah a receipt for her parents' tax records. "Make sure you specify an amount when you get home."

Sitting in the car waiting at the light, Sarah took a look at the form. Everything had been filled in except the donation amount. It looked like a big blank spot on the paper, like it was obvious that there was nothing there. How do you put a value on a life? Sarah asked herself turning the corner and heading for home. It would be another week before she could walk back into Jenna's room.

CHAPTER 13

That summer at home after Jenna's death was filled with firsts. The first time home since Jenna died. The first family gathering, Mother's Day, since Jenna died. The list went on. And then there was the first trip to the grocery store without Jenna.

A Saturday evening tradition at the McCall house was to eat breakfast for dinner. Arlene did it up with bacon, eggs, and huge stacks of pancakes. Matt didn't come anymore but even when Jenna was home and Sarah was away at college, her mother still cooked it anyway.

"I would never forgive her if she didn't make me my Saturday night special," Frank McCall had joked as Arlene handed him a stack of pancakes for the table.

There was little that felt part of the past now. It felt like everything had sprung forward even though Sarah didn't feel like springing forward, at least not at that time. But when she took a bite of those pancakes, a recipe she never could replicate and let them melt in her mouth, she felt herself drawn back through the years. First it was back to her and Jenna's high school days when they would invite their friends over after swim meets and tennis matches so their friends could be part of the Saturday night tradition. To the junior high years when they struggled with believing they were too cool to be part of something so...family. So traditional. To elementary school when they fought over who got the syrup first. All those years. All those meals consumed. All those memories over a meal they referred to as "breakfast for dinner" or "b for d."

"Oh dear," her mother said, her head stuck in the refrigerator, only her back end protruding. Sarah could hear her sorting through plastic packages and moving jars around. "I can't believe this. I'm out of bacon."

"Gasp," her father called from the table where he was completing the *Chicago Tribune* crossword puzzle for that day. "You better go get some."

Arlene McCall looked at Sarah sitting at the table flipping through a celebrity gossip magazine.

"Will you?" Sarah looked at her mother. If she didn't go, there would be no pancakes. She wasn't so much thinking about the bacon. Just the pancakes. But her dad wanted the bacon. Sarah got up and looked for her sandals.

"You can take my car," her mother said pointing to the keys on the table.

Sarah walked outside. The station wagon didn't have many miles left on it. She knew her mother's rational thinking would win out. "You could take the station wagon," she would have said, "but dinner is already running late and if you get stuck, you'll have the bacon and we'll have the pancakes."

Sarah placed her hand on the hood of the station wagon, walking by it. Her father said he was going to get rid of it soon. He planned to do that once Jenna left for college in the fall anyway, he said.

But it wasn't until she was halfway to the grocery store, a place she didn't have to think about how to get to, it was as if she and the car were connected and it knew what to do, that she remembered she hadn't been there since Jenna died. After the funeral, the house was filled with food, enough that her mother was giving it away to the neighbors. "You can't freeze deli sandwiches," she said, handing a platter to the Browns one evening. "And you can't freeze potato salad," she said, handing a bowl to the Smiths another evening. She held onto all the lasagnas and the casseroles, feeding her and Frank for weeks after. "I wish you were home to help us eat all this food," she had said on the phone to Sarah. Sarah couldn't think about food. She wished someone would cook for her. Why didn't her mother offer her any of those casseroles to take back with her? Why didn't anyone offer her a lasagna? She was a college student. Lost in the shuffle, she felt.

Now she was on her way to the grocery store, the very place she and her sister loved to visit. They knew exactly where everything they needed for their oatmeal cookies was placed and waiting for them to purchase. When they remodeled the store, during Sarah's freshman year of college, it was Jenna who called her in a panic. "They remodeled the store! I can't find anything!" It was those moments that Sarah thought Jenna couldn't live without her. And as menial as the remodeling of the grocery store seemed, it was part of their time together and she wished she had been home to explore the store in its updated version for their future purchases with her sister. Instead, Jenna showed her around when she arrived back in town for that Thanksgiving.

"Makes no sense," Jenna had said, "why the raisins are in the cereal aisle now. Who is the doofus who decides these things?"

Saturday evening filled the store with a variety of people. Sarah tried to concentrate. "Bacon, bacon, bacon," she muttered under her breath to remind herself why she was there. No oatmeal, no raisins, no flour, not even sugar. Bacon. She couldn't remember ever buying bacon before in her life.

And she couldn't remember being in the store without Jenna. After walking past the cashier lanes with the magazines showing celebrities they would make fun of, to the back of the store to the refrigerated meat section, and grabbing the bacon, Sarah walked through the cereal aisle, where the oatmeal sat on several shelves waiting to be bought. She didn't need it now. At the time she didn't think she ever could make the cookies again. It felt like that part of her, the part that wanted to make cookies and watch baseball, had died with her sister. There was no sense that it ever would come back.

Instead of driving directly home, Sarah took the long way. She wasn't sure why she did it. Maybe she just needed to be out a little longer. If her mother asked her why she was gone so long she could tell her the line was long in the store. She'd make up something lame and her mother probably wouldn't know differently. It didn't matter.

She turned right out of the store parking lot and headed toward downtown Cedarville. The closer she drove to downtown, the older the houses became. The subdivisions had blended into a different time, where housing was different, where life was different. Sarah almost felt as if her own life represented the same change. There was before Jenna died and there was after Jenna died. Just like in Cedarville where Willow Drive separated the new part of town with the old, Jenna's death did the same for Sarah's life.

They were lucky to live in Cedarville. Sarah always laughed at the sign on the way into town that said, "A thriving community." And it was. But it was with one less member, one whose death shook up many people; it didn't feel it thrived as much as it had before. Her mother said she head a rumor that the school added suicide prevention trainings for staff after Jenna's suicide.

"Fear we'll sue," her father interjected. "Don't think they are that paranoid about losing another student so much as they are we'll sue."

"Why would you sue?" Sarah asked, puzzled that they were having the conversation.

Frank McCall put his newspaper down and rubbed his eyes. "We could sue because the school didn't see any signs. It's happened in other places. But what's the point? We can't bring Jenna back anyway."

She turned to her mother. "Why weren't they trained in suicide prevention before?"

Arlene McCall shook her head. "I don't know. I guess no one is until it happens. Maybe that's a good thing that can come from Jenna's suicide, that other people won't miss the signs and another life won't be lost."

What were the signs? Sarah still didn't understand any of it. She vaguely remembered high school health class where they discussed suicide. They watched what had been one of those Tuesday night television movies where a kid, always a boy, ends his life and his parents struggle to understand. Then there's always the sister who feels like no one is listening to her. Sarah didn't think she wanted to watch the movie now. It would be better if she could write her own.

She circled one of the downtown blocks then headed home. That was enough for one day. The thought of trying to understand the signs of suicide made her too sad. From her high school health class she remembered something about giving things away. Looking at Jenna's room, that hadn't been done. They must have missed something, but at that time, Sarah couldn't see it.

*****

Several years later, during Sarah's only trip to visit her parents in Florida, she stood at the edge of the Gulf of Mexico. It was as if she stood in multiple points of time. Part of her heard the voices, the giggles of her and Jenna as they played in the ocean when they were in elementary school on a spring break trip with their parents. Matt taught them how to ride waves and they rushed toward them, trying to become one with the waves as they carried them back to shore. They searched for shells, picking up anything they found, something they would laugh about years later when they found a plastic hotel laundry bag filled with all those shells that their mother had kept for them.

~ Sisters: The Karma Twist ~

"These are crappy shells," Sarah and Jenna would laugh then. "What were we thinking?"

"I just saved them all," their mother would say in her defense.

The giggles were gone, somewhere in the background now of where Sarah stood. She felt her feet merge with the wet sand as the Gulf water rolled toward her and then pulled back. She looked across her, to the other side she couldn't see, to the shores of Texas. So far away. That's where Jenna was. So far away. The power of the Gulf reminded her how small she was in the scheme of life. The ocean could drown someone. The ocean could drown the Titantic. Was Jenna's life that small in the puzzle of every-thing? she wondered, picking up a shell and throwing it as far as she could into the horizon. It felt like the unanswered questions kept coming. Sarah wondered when the day would come when she would stop asking them. Or maybe she would get some answers.

CHAPTER 14

"I need more cookies," Mark said, this time stopping Sarah in the front office where she dropped off her daily attendance reports.

"Don't you think you should stop by my office asking me that where I can write it down?" she teased him, slipping the forms into the slot by the attendance secretary's desk.

"I looked for you but you weren't there. The boy in your classroom said you were here."

And so it went. There were weekly orders. Sarah learned the aisles in her local grocery store that held the items she needed. The very items she hadn't bought in years. The items that had tied her to Jenna for so long. It didn't feel bad. It felt weird at first to buy them more often than she and Jenna ever did. And in larger quantities. She began to consider joining a membership club. Maybe she would need the vats of butter she and Jenna joked about.

"Are you serious?" Barbara asked her when Sarah had shown up for her weekly dinner at Barbara's house. "You're making cookies again? Then you need to make some for me."

Sarah surprised herself, and Barbara, when she grabbed a piece of paper from the counter next to Barbara's calendar and began to look for a pen. "What do you want?"

"Really? Seriously?" Barbara's mouth gaped open. The ponytail on top of her head shook when she spoke. "The best cookies in the world are back in business?"

"Yes." Sarah laughed. She didn't think it was a big deal. It felt good. That's all she cared about.

"And this is because of this baseball dude?" Barbara was thinking, Sarah could tell. It was as if the mixer in her head put it all together. "I need to meet this guy. He obviously gets something the rest of us couldn't figure out."

That Sunday, Mark sat down at the bar opposite her kitchen, a first, with Sarah realizing she had never asked him to stay. "Conference play ends next week you know," he said. Usually he peeked under the foil at the cookies but not today.

"I heard," she said. "I make my kids listen to the announcements."

"You haven't been to a game," he noted, leaning toward her.

"I know." Was she glad he noticed? Did she want to go?

"It would mean a lot for you to be at our last home game."

"To whom?" She felt the script playing out. There wasn't room for description. This was conversation. Or was it banter? She wished she had a thesaurus. Something made her want to look it up.

"To the kids. To the booster club." He paused and looked at her. "And to me."

Sarah nodded, knowing he had uttered an appropriate answer. "Name the time and I'll be there. I don't have to bring more cookies though, do I?"

"No, you're off the hook until next week when we start regional play."

"Pretty convenient you're hosting," she said.

"Pretty convenient you know that we're hosting," he countered, getting up and grabbing his keys and sunglasses.

"I told you, I make my kids listen to the announcements. Chess club and everything."

"He likes you," Barbara said to Sarah at dinner that week, the night before the game.

"How do you know?" Sarah scoffed, taking another bite of the lasagna. "I bake cookies that help him make more money for his team. It's not like I'm getting rich off it."

"Please, girl, it's my intuition. I know these things. He likes you. He wants to show off the hottest teacher in school at the baseball game and let everyone know that he's the one who asked her to come to the game."

"Wear one of those tennis skirts," her husband Jeff suggested, a piece of garlic bread near his mouth. "You look pretty good in one of those."

"Oh," Barbara said, disgusted. "If Sarah hadn't been my friend for so long and didn't know you so well, I'd tell you how gross you are. But at least she knows to expect this sort of thing from you."

"At least it's a compliment," Sarah reminded her friend. "And it's coming from a grown man rather than a sixteen-year-old boy."

"They don't really say that to you do?" Barbara looked a little nervous. "Do they?"

Sarah laughed and took another bite of her dinner. She never answered.

*****

It rained so hard before the conference tournament that the fields at Mill West were too wet and the game was canceled. Sarah hoped none of the kids heard her sigh of relief that afternoon when Principal McGann made the announcement. They lost in the first round of regional play, ending the season for Mark's team earlier than he had planned.

*****

It usually happened the first week of classes. Sarah liked to spend time getting to know her students. It wasn't always so easy. Some preferred she didn't know them. But she knew that the majority liked the attention she bestowed on them. Sarah hadn't forgotten her own high school years. She knew everyone needed attention. She and Jenna, and her brother to some degree although he was gone from home by then, all fought for parental resources, mainly attention. The McCalls did a good job making sure each girl got what she needed although Sarah knew now they doubted the job they had done since Jenna had died.

That aside, she loved being singled out by teachers in school. Everyone wants to feel important, she realized in the two years after Jenna died.

It was an outgoing girl, the kind who did all the extra credit and volunteered every answer so much that Sarah had to turn a blind eye to her, giving the other students a chance to participate (something they usually didn't want, preferring to let the girl answer all the questions, but Sarah knew how those games were played since she had played them in high school as well). It was this girl who raised her hand that first or second day of class and asked, "Ms. McCall, why did you become a teacher?"

No one knew that she had lost her sister, particularly to suicide. Sarah didn't tell anyone because she had so few answers. Five years after her sister's death, she was teaching and it didn't feel right to announce that that was the reason her life had changed. How could students who were sixteen and seventeen understand something that had happened when they were eleven or twelve? That was eons ago for them. Sarah decided it was best not to tread those waters.

They all needed to feel important, Sarah reminded herself even on the roughest days, the days when she wondered what else she could do with her life. The days when she went from school to tennis to home to get ready for the next day. The days when the papers to grade stood so high on her desk that when her students left, sometimes she cried because she didn't know what else to do.

No one knew why Jenna ended her life. She took all those answers with her. There were few ideas, Sarah knowing that the best guess was probably her own relating to Jenna's fear for the future. Jenna had lots of people: a slew of friends, teachers, staff, their parents, her friends' parents, the list went on, that she could reach out to. But she didn't and that made Sarah question what was missing. Someone must have been missing. That person who could have made a difference wasn't there.

Sarah didn't expect to walk into a classroom and think her students would reach out to her. She hoped in some way, particularly over those first few weeks of school, she could instill some hope for life that they could be anything they wanted to be.

She wanted to create an atmosphere where they felt safe, where they knew that no matter what they said in class, Sarah would support it in some way, even when it wasn't the answer she sought. She wanted them to know that, while they might feel awkward and not believe they belong, some day that would change. She often shook her head thinking of this, never believing that Jenna ever felt awkward. Sarah thought she was the awkward one. Jenna had more "zest" (the word she often thought of) for life than Sarah did. Apparently she used it to hide something and the day came where she couldn't hide it anymore. Sarah didn't want her students to ever feel that way.

* * * * *

~ Sisters: The Karma Twist ~

The evening after Jenna's funeral, Sarah felt exhaustion she never knew existed. She knew physical exhaustion well from tennis but this was physical and mental exhaustion. She had no idea she could feel physically exhausted from standing around talking about her sister's unexplainable death. The day started at the funeral home, took them to the cemetery, and rounded out at Jenna's favorite restaurant, The Giant Gyro, a small Greek place in town run by two brothers.

"Not the normal way to do a funeral," her mother lamented, watching everyone order, but there was a sense of satisfaction on her face that she knew Jenna would have approved. "Definitely not like any funeral ever before in my family."

"Not like it was a normal death," Sarah said, as if her mother had to be reminded.

"We're glad we could do this," Basil, one of the owners said, his arm reaching around Arlene McCall's shoulders.

"We thank you so much," Sarah's mother said.

One year it had been Jenna's goal to eat there once a week. She had succeeded until November when she got sick right after the swimming season ended.

"You have to take me there," she begged their mother, who continued to shake her head and tell Jenna no. When she left the room, Jenna turned and begged Sarah who stood next to her bed. She grabbed Sarah's hand. Sarah tried to pull it away, not wanting her sister's fever. "You have to take me," Jenna seethed. Sarah wondered if her sister was high on the Giant Gyro and couldn't come off it.

"How?" Sarah asked. "How am I going to get you past Mom?"

"Stupid, she doesn't come home from work until we're home from school two hours. Maybe you can ask her to stop at the grocery store. No, I'll ask her to get me something. Some feta cheese. That'll throw her off."

For being sick, Sarah thought her sister was in pretty good mental shape. But Sarah also understood her sister's need to fulfill a goal and Sarah didn't want to deprive her of that. She was just six weeks, six measly visits to the Giant Gyro, from achieving her goal. How could she miss it now because she had a fever?

The next afternoon, Jenna was ready as soon as Sarah got home from school. She stood at the front door wrapped in a blanket, her team sweats on, and her big purple fuzzy slippers on her feet.

"You know you look really bad, right?" Sarah asked, not sure if she should make fun of or empathize with her sister.

"I don't care," Jenna snapped. "Just get me to my gyro sandwich and feta cheese."

Watching Jenna slurp down her sandwich, the sauce sliding down all parts of her hand, was enough to make Sarah know, no matter what their mother said if she found out, it was worth taking Jenna out for that sandwich.

And it was only after Jenna died did she tell her parents what happened that day.

"We thought she never met her goal," her mother said, shaking her head. "At least now I know I didn't cause her suicide by not taking her."

Sarah looked at her mother. "Seriously, you thought that?"

Arlene McCall looked sadly at Sarah. "You have no idea how many 'things' I've been thinking that I wished I had done differently. Maybe I should have picked her up in her crib when she was crying all those nights. Maybe I should have bought her that Barbie doll she cried so much for at the store that we had to leave." Sarah could see the sadness in her mother's face. It aged her in just a few short days. These "things" were important to her mother and Sarah didn't dare make any other comments. She hugged her instead before someone else came up to talk to her. Sarah left, looking for the feta cheese.

The Giant Gyro closed down the year after Jenna died. Sarah was kind of glad she wasn't in town to drive by what was now called O' Slice of Pizza. It wasn't the same without "the brothers" but they were tired of serving gyros and retired to Florida. Sometimes Sarah liked to think they were sad about Jenna dying and couldn't make gyro sandwiches anymore. But that was the five year old in her talking. She knew she'd also be tired of making gyro sandwiches every day after twenty years.

Change happened after Jenna died and would continue to happen. It wasn't just the repaving of the streets or the planting of new trees, it was that stores closed, that television shows ended, that life went on and Jenna remained a seventeen year old. Sarah turned twenty-five, she turned thirty, yet Jenna remained seventeen. She would turn forty, then fifty. Still Jenna would be seventeen.

Sarah wondered when she reached Heaven, would she be old and Jenna young? What would they have in common?

On the night of Jenna's funeral, Sarah was glad when everyone left and the house was quiet. She didn't realize that the same silence that brought her comfort now would bother her when she returned home for the summer, and for every trip to the house after that.

*****

Sarah stood in front of her parent's house, a glass of orange juice in one hand, the newspaper in the other. It was not yet 7:00 am on a summer Saturday, the shadows long across the lawns and into the street. She missed those few mornings when she was young and she and Jenna would get up and ride their bikes around, knowing only the adults in the neighborhood were up.

Now she was one of those adults, not quite old enough to have a family and home of her own, but old enough to be up early and be part of that landscape. It was four months past Jenna's suicide and life didn't feel the same. She knew it wouldn't be the same again although she kept wishing that one day she would wake up and it would be.

Standing in front of the only house she had known in her life, reminded of the life she shared with Jenna, and the life of the entire McCall family, she wondered what other people thought. Her dad opened the front door, looking for the newspaper, she knew, and she walked inside, thinking about how she was going to get the sports section before he did.

CHAPTER 15

No one loved to celebrate Jenna's birthday more than Jenna. She often joked that September was her birthday month and that they could all celebrate all month long, mostly by giving Jenna gifts. The actual date of her birth, the seventeenth, was always busy for Sarah. When she was in college, she attended classes; in graduate school she was taught and attended classes. When she graduated, she taught and coached. But until Jenna died, that day was all Jenna's. If Sarah wasn't at home, like she wasn't for the three years of Jenna's birthday, she always sent her balloons or tried to think of something silly to do for her sister.

Sometimes she got her dad involved (her mom often wanted no part of it) and they plotted together by filling the station wagon with Styrofoam peanuts (Sarah was still shocked that that actually was *his* idea) or having a singing telegram delivered to her fourth period class (she couldn't believe the school let them get away with that one) her senior year, months before her death. What mattered was that they wanted Jenna to know she was special and that was her day.

Sarah had been planning for a year what she would do for Jenna's freshman year at college. It would be much easier there in some ways. She could have just about anything delivered to her dorm. The tough part was that she didn't have her dad to help (nor would she know any of Jenna's friends at college), but the possibilities were endless. And although Jenna was still on the fence between two schools when she died, Sarah also had thought about surprising her sister for what would have been her eighteenth birthday.

Instead, her eighteenth birthday was coming and there would be no plans. Sarah couldn't go home to place a birthday cake on her sister's gravestone. She was tempted to do it anyway and sit there and eat half the cake by herself. If any other person had died, that would have been Jenna's idea. "Hey, let's get a cake and eat it at the cemetery." Sarah would have cringed at the idea but Jenna would have added, "Oh, it'll be fun. It'll be a great way to remember so-and-so."

Sarah wasn't going home until Thanksgiving. And thus September 17 turned into just an ordinary day. The world didn't stop because Jenna wasn't in it and it was her birthday (along with millions of other people). Sarah wished that for two minutes everyone would stop and recognize that her sister was gone. But then how could that happen for everyone who lost someone? The world would never start spinning again. Life wasn't meant to stop, even when someone died.

Instead, Sarah trekked to downtown Madison and bought a cake. It was just a small cake, the kind one or two people might share, the kind Sarah expected that Jenna would have picked out if someone else had died. Although the leaves started to turn, it was still warm enough for shorts. Sarah walked out with the cake and a plastic fork in one hand, her backpack in the other, and sat at one of the stone tables in front of the bakery. She opened the box and took a deep breath, thinking maybe she should have bought a candle. No, she thought, pulling the cake out, she'd just eat as much as she'd want and throw away the rest.

It was a white cake with raspberry filling. Sarah knew she was lucky to find Jenna's favorite, especially because it was later in the day. For all she knew, all the people who had birthdays on September 17 all liked the same kind of cake. She threw the box away and sat with the cake in front of her. Butter cream flowers in blue and yellow dotted the cake.

Sarah looked around. Was there something strange about a girl eating a cake by herself? It didn't matter. She tried to remember that Jenna would say it was silly to worry about what others thought and dug her fork into the cake. As she took her first bite, only getting frosting, she thought about the bakery. It was a little Mom and Pop place that had been there for years, probably catering to the college crowd that got married as soon as graduation ended. She hadn't been in there before. She wondered if that would have been the kind of bakery she and Jenna would have had.

She slipped her fork in deeper and reached the cake and the filling this time. The retro styling of the bakery gave it a homey feel. It reminded her of the bakeries they went to near their grandparents' house when they grew up. She couldn't wrap her mind around two opposing ideas. One was the traditional kind of bakery they grew up with, like the one by their grandparents' house, but then she wondered if maybe she and Jenna would have done something more trendy that felt retro but modern.

Eating more cake, she let the thought drop. She knew she'd never find out these answers. Sarah pushed the plate away after a few more bites. She felt the sugar, both in her bloodstream and on her teeth. She'd eaten about a quarter of it. She threw the rest away, not wanting to explain to her room-mates what she did with a cake, of all things. "Why did you buy it and eat part of it? It looks like you jabbed a fork in it repeatedly. Why didn't you cut it with a knife like a normal person?" It wasn't worth it.

She had celebrated Jenna's birthday and it was time to move on. At least for now. Sarah didn't want to think about Jenna for a while. She needed a little laughter, she needed something to focus on. She headed back to campus for one of her nutrition labs. Nutrition might not be funny but at least she could focus on proteins and carbohydrates for a while.

*****

The house was quiet without Jenna. There was no doubt about that. Sarah missed the noise of her sister flying down the stairs, usually followed by herself. She missed their banter, even on their crabbiest mornings when they acted as if they didn't want to be sisters anymore. Sarah longed for the arguing because it meant Jenna was alive.

Sorting out a box of papers at the dining room table, Sarah rubbed her eyes and wished for sound. Her parents were still at work. It was 2:30 in the afternoon. The sun shone brightly through the front windows. The Cubs played on television, she was sure. There was no way she could bring herself to turn the television on. Or make oatmeal cookies. Baseball was gone, the bakery was gone, Jenna was gone.

*****

In those first days and months she clung to a shiny lime green folder filled with cards and memories of her sister. The folder, now worn, still stood upright in the bookshelf with all her teaching materials that weren't in her classroom. There was a tear in the front of it, probably from moving it to Wisconsin, to Kansas, and then back to Illinois, between her parents' house and everywhere else she lived. She didn't open it up often like she had in the past. It didn't have the same meaning for her now as it did ten years ago when it helped her cling to the memories of her sister. The many cards from friends sat in the front of the folder with newspaper clippings, Jenna's obituary, right behind them. There were a few photos although most them were in a photo album that rested next to the folder on the bookshelf.

~ Sisters: The Karma Twist ~

There was little left of Jenna's life now. Her room had been cleaned out, what they didn't keep given away. Who would need her shoes that wouldn't fit anyone else in the family or anyone else they knew? And then her parents moved, leaving the house completely for another family.

"Maybe we should have it smudged," Sarah had said, standing in its emptiness, her shoes echoing underneath her on the wood floor in the upstairs hallway.

"What's that?" her mother asked, checking for the millionth time that she had removed everything from the closets.

"It's a Native American thing," Sarah said, taking her hands out of the pockets of her leather jacket as if using her hands to demonstrate something she didn't know would help it make sense. "They do it to get rid of anything bad."

Arlene McCall shot her daughter a look and Sarah knew she shouldn't have said it. "And rid this house of the happy memories of your sister?"

Sarah wanted to tell her that wasn't what she meant. She didn't want to rid the house of her sister at all. She just wanted to rid the house of the fact that Jenna had ended her life there. This wasn't about smothering out the happy memories. That wasn't what a smudge was about. But she knew her mother wouldn't understand. She dropped the subject and helped her look through the closets and cabinets one last time.

The house wasn't theirs anymore as it had been for twenty years. It was ready for a new family, one with young children, just like the McCalls had been when they moved in. Sarah took one last long look into each room, letting the memories fall off her as she did. The walls had been painted, erasing Jenna's lavender paint and Sarah's sky blue motif. All the walls were some form of white, ready like new canvases for the new family. But the fact that it wasn't theirs anymore, that it was empty, and now devoid of the majority of the memories, took some of the sting out of leaving.

*****

It was no secret that Jenna had ended her life at the house on 116 Cedar Lane. As she had been told by everyone, the police and the medical examiner parked in front of the house for several hours had turned out everyone in the neighborhood. People gathered on the sidewalks when Jenna's body was taken out.

"You mean, like a tribute or because they were curious?" she asked Matt who had been there.

"I always thought it was more because they were curious. It's not every day that something like that happens in the neighborhood."

"Thank God," Sarah said under her breath.

She wondered how many people, of the ones who stood out there, knew them, knew anything about their family, and knew Jenna. Over the years, the neighborhood had changed. Everyone grew up, some families moved away. It wasn't as it had been when they grew up and knew everyone. And now everyone would only remember Jenna for her final act. Her suicide.

It bothered Sarah and often she wished there was some way to clear her sister's name. She wanted people to know Jenna as the whole person, not just the girl who hung herself in her bedroom. She wanted them to know how creative she was, how much fun she was. The very things her school classmates remembered about her. Their disbelief about Jenna's death was due to what they saw from her school. They would not remember her in the body bag wheeled out of the house on a gurney.

Sarah wished she had been there. She wished she could have held up a bullhorn and yelled out to everyone that just because her sister had ended her life didn't make her a bad person, a sick person, someone who wasn't loved. But she didn't think of this until years after Jenna had died.

*****

As the second anniversary had loomed on Sarah, she found herself thinking about it without realizing what she was doing. She often rolled a pencil between the palm of her hand and her desk at KU. Her officemate, Kayla, would reach over and put her hand on top of Sarah's.

"Hey, where are you?" Kayla learned to ask when she saw that Sarah wasn't doing it on purpose.

Sarah shook her head, closed her eyes, and reopened them. She didn't know where she'd been. She looked at Kayla and shrugged her shoulders.

"You're lucky I'm tolerable of your weird behavior," Kayla joked. "If I hadn't lost my dad to suicide, I wouldn't have any clue what you're going through."

~ Sisters: The Karma Twist ~

One of the few bonds Sarah found in those first years after Jenna's death was Kayla. Her dad killed himself when she was thirteen, on the cusp of the teen years, and suddenly without the man who should have been guiding and leading her. Kayla would push her chair back from her desk and throw her feet on it, waiting for Sarah to say something about what she'd just been thinking about.

"One day you'll finally tell me. I just know it."

"The second anniversary is in two weeks," Sarah finally blurted out, dropping her pencil to the floor as she said. When she got back up from retrieving it, Kayla nodded her head. "I think it's worse than the first one because I know what to expect."

"That's all you had to tell me, girl. I get it."

Sarah nodded, as if she admitted guilt to stealing something.

"You don't have to hide this from me. The key is the anticipation is much worse than the day. Make some plans. Whatever you do though, don't not make plans." She stopped herself and thought for a minute. "Is that a double negative?" She turned back to Sarah, "Doesn't matter, you know what I mean."

It was hard for Sarah to make plans that year though. She taught that day, both of her freshman English 101 classes. There wouldn't be much time with office hours between. The year before she had a day off from classes and went for a long bike ride, something she knew Jenna would have approved of, even in February. Sarah had needed the cold wind chapping her face. It made her feel alive.

The night before the anniversary, Sarah couldn't help but reflect back to where she was that night the two years before. At a party with Celia and her then-boyfriend Pete. She looked forward to Friday, the next day after a long week. Instead, she drove home for Jenna's funeral.

Standing in front of her class the morning of the anniversary, all those long faces, "dead fish heads" as Kayla often called them, waiting for her to inspire them. Sarah felt uninspired herself though. She regretted not canceling class. She didn't want to stay in bed either. Somehow she had to discuss the basics of essay writing, the topic she promised them on this day. Not a topic she wanted to discuss but their papers showed signs of needing help. This would have been a better day for some sort of discussion that didn't involve her doing all the talking.

By the end of the class, the dead fish heads filing out, Sarah was worn out. She wondered how she could make it through office hours and then another 50-minute session. This was a day when the students would have questions.

Sarah hated to replay that day in her mind. The only word, besides sad, that came to mind was "jolty." She always forgot to actually look it up and see if it was a word. The day didn't fit together. She didn't feel right, especially as she approached the hour of Jenna's death. The time the death certificate recorded was 2:13 pm. She never understood where the number came from but never had the courage to ask about it either.

Her second class started at 2:00 pm. She wished she could put off class until 2:15. She thought about staying away. She thought about running away. Surely there was some way around this. But the more she thought about it, the worse she felt. The anxiety began to rip through her.

She dragged herself out of the office and down the hall to the lecture hall. 2:05. Her second round of dead fish heads waited. And quietly. Almost as if they knew.

Sarah took a deep breath; all she could do was start the essay lecture. She couldn't keep her eyes off the clock though. It was one of those moments that when Sarah thought back on it in her life, she wanted to curl up deeper under her comforter as if the world wasn't there. Because if the world wasn't there, then it never happened, right?

It was uncomfortable. She ached as the minutes went by. And finally when 2:13 hit, she realized it meant…nothing. Nothing changed. The same students still stared at her expecting inspiring words about how to write essays. Her world didn't topple over. She survived. And although she wasn't in a hurry to do it again the next year, she knew that she could when it was time.

She hoped the next year she planned a little better.

CHAPTER 16

While Sarah and Jenna bonded over making cookies and their shared love for baseball, there was one other place where they explored their daily lives together. The family station wagon.

When Sarah turned sixteen, her parents promptly went out and bought a new car. Frank McCall teased his daughter, telling her that he was buying her a convertible. Sarah knew this wasn't true and tried her best to ignore him. They didn't buy Matt a car, instead giving him their grandfather's 1960s car. It was beat up but that meant Matt loved it even more. He spent hours in the driveway cleaning it, despite all its rusted glory, changing the oil, and keeping up with it. His friends loved it because it, well, it was a car and none of the others had one. He drove it until it died one day in a grocery store parking lot when he was in college. Then Frank rewarded his son with a new car.

Sarah dreaded that she would meet the same fate although she wasn't sure where the car would come from.

"We must have some uncle who has a piece of shit in his garage that we don't know about," she lamented to Jenna one night in Jenna's room shortly before her birthday in July.

"Well, I hope it's not Uncle Dwight," Jenna said, turning up her nose. "He's kind of gross so you know his car is kind of gross."

"He's not really our uncle anyway," Sarah reminded her. "He was married to Mom's friend Doreen. And aren't they getting divorced anyway?"

Jenna's head was upside down, her ponytail hanging to the floor from the top of her bed. "How do you know all this?"

Sarah sat at the head of Jenna's bed, deciding which of her sister's stuffed animals she liked the best. "I heard Mom on the phone with Doreen, trying to calm her down. I don't know why Doreen was so upset though. That guy was gross. And to think it was her second husband." She watched her sister although she could only see her body and not her head. "Doesn't that make you dizzy?"

Jenna pulled herself back up on the bed. "Nah." She sat on the other side of the bed from Sarah and grabbed the worn stuffed bear out of Sarah's hands. "Be nice to Mr. Brown, please."

Never in a million years did Sarah expect her parents to hand her the keys to the blue station wagon. The station wagon that took them everywhere throughout her childhood. The one whose backseat that she and Jenna simultaneously fought and played in. The one that took them to CCD, swim practice, Girl Scouts, and brought home every grocery that fed the family all those years.

But hand Sarah the keys to the station was just what they did on the afternoon of Sarah's birthday after she passed the driving test and received that small card that meant freedom to every teenager in the United States.

What they hadn't told Sarah, or Jenna, was that they had bought a new car the previous afternoon. Instead of parking it in their driveway, it was next door at the Smith house. After Arlene brought Sarah home with her license, Jenna jubilantly flew out of the house to see if it was true.

"Are we really free to go to the grocery store any time we want? When can we drive to a Cubs game?" She ignored her mother's frowns behind Sarah.

"We'll see," was all Sarah said, trying to keep her excitement under wraps. She could feel that famous frown penetrating her back and tried to warn Jenna. Jenna wouldn't stop though.

Their dad walked out of the house and joined the three of them in the driveway on the hot, humid afternoon that none of them noticed. "I take it you passed?" he asked.

"Of course I did," Sarah told him with a hint of snide in her voice. "Why wouldn't I?"

"Your brother didn't the first time," Arlene reminded Sarah.

"And you gave him a piece of crap to drive. No wonder."

Frank reached into his pocket and pulled out a set of keys. "And we're giving you this." Two keys were secured together with a grocery store keychain. The back of it had the Cubs emblem. It was a giveaway from a game.

"What car?" Sarah asked, anxiously letting them fall from his fingers into her cupped hands. She turned them over to inspect them. Impala. Impala what? She looked up to see her dad pointing at the station wagon she had just climbed out of. The very one she just drove home from the motor vehicle department. "The station wagon?" She wasn't sure if she was happy or disappointed. Most of all though, she was confused. "What will Mom drive?"

Her father then pointed at a white sedan in the Smith driveway. It hadn't been there prior to the day before but Sarah didn't think much of it. She didn't pay attention (or care) what the Smiths did. "We bought a new car yesterday."

"Yippee!" Jenna exclaimed, jumping around. "We have a car!"

"Uh, I have a car," Sarah reminded her. It was definitely a step up from what her brother got. It wasn't new. She wasn't expecting new. But it was a car. It had four wheels. It ran. Really, what more could she ask for?

"Can I take it out?" She looked at her parents hesitantly.

Now her mother smiled, the first smile since Sarah emerged from the line with her license in hand at the motor vehicle department. "Go. Not too far, but go."

"Let's go to the grocery store," Jenna cried, running in the house to get her flip flops.

That afternoon, that trip to the grocery store just a mile away, where they bought a new package of oatmeal, would be the start of a new bond between them. No longer did they have to ask to go to the store at 7:00 pm when they realized they were out of butter to make cookies for that 9:00 pm game on the West Coast. No longer did they have to beg Arlene to take them to school when they wanted to sleep in fifteen minutes (not that it mattered when Jenna had morning swim practice though). They were free.

The discussions they shared changed as their interests grew with their maturity as high school students. They weren't always in the car together. Sometimes Jenna had to go early and Sarah usually had to stay late, but there was enough time in the spring when both of them weren't involved in any sports, that they shared their daily lives in a new way. A way that Sarah missed when she went to college.

She didn't realize how much she enjoyed sharing what had happened during the day at school with Jenna. She had her friends but it was different with Jenna. And there was her sister experiencing her first crushes on the brothers of boys that Sarah knew. All she wanted was to protect her sister from the boys she knew might hurt her. But a part of her also knew that she couldn't completely ever protect her.

It was as painful as watching Jenna do her first penny drops at Mary Adams's house two blocks away. Mary's dad had built her a set of bars in the backyard, bars that were long gone and now would probably be considered a playing hazard. Mary went first doing a dime drop, starting at the top of the bars, falling backward, and then swinging until she released her legs and flew in the air, landing on her feet. Sarah went second, having conquered her fear of doing the dime drop as well. It would be Jenna' first time. Sarah held her sister's hands as she hung upside down.

Sarah could see Jenna's fear. She was about seven and the only reason she was there was because Sarah knew she wanted to do what Sarah did. Sarah also knew that her mother would probably kill her if anything happened to Jenna. Whether Jenna wanted her to or not, she was going to hold Jenna's hands and guide her down. All Jenna had to do was let her legs go. And trust Sarah that she wouldn't let go of her hands.

Sarah swung her sister, slowly twice and quicker the third time calling out the number of each swing– "One...two...THREE!" And with that, Jenna did as she was instructed and came flying to the ground, somehow managing to land on her feet. It wasn't a perfect landing, one that wouldn't win her an Olympic medal. But Sarah was happy. No broken bones, no grass stains on her pants.

And it was the same for the conversations in the car. She wanted to protect her sister from any pain, from hurt, yet she was smart enough to know that she needed to let her travel her own road. She didn't think that Jenna would end her life far too soon before she really understood the rewards of all that early hurt.

After Jenna died, Sarah missed the routine of their lives even more. When she came home from college there was no Jenna excited to see her, no Jenna to hang out with, no Jenna to tell about dates and school. No Jenna to share her life with. She found herself many times almost running to the phone to call her sister before realizing that there was no Jenna to call anymore. No Jenna to drive the station wagon that had been handed to her when Sarah left for Wisconsin, her parents afraid that it wouldn't make it over the state border more than once.

CHAPTER 17

Everyone has one of those shelves in their kitchen, the one at the top of the cabinet that you don't often see what's up there. Usually you think about it once a year, at the holidays when you're having a party and you need those extra wine glasses or coffee cups. You pull the ladder up to the counter and travel halfway to the kitchen ceiling to see that there is a layer of dust on everything and you'll have to clean anything before you use it. Plus there's only an hour before the party starts.

Sarah usually glanced up at her "cabinet in the sky," as she often called it, several times a year. If the light hit the kitchen just right, the light from the sun would bounce off the glasses as if they were smiling.

But Sarah wasn't smiling when she craned her neck and saw the two large ice tea glasses with the Christmas trees painted on the sides. Marshall Fields Christmas, 1991.

"I don't get it," Sarah had said, opening the set at Christmas that year, Jenna's last Christmas.

"It's for when you have someone to share them with," Jenna had exclaimed. She was so excited that she almost fell backward from where she sat on the floor with her legs crossed. Only Jenna could almost fall backward on the floor with her legs crossed.

It was a great idea, Sarah knew that. But it hadn't worked out that way. Of course, it was possible that Jenna had no idea at Christmas that she planned to end her life early in the next year. Now Sarah glanced up and saw them, next to the dainty coffee cups that belonged to her grandmother's china, and wondered if she would ever have the chance to use them.

She should have with Ken. She remembered taking them out of the cabinet two Christmases later, her first at Kansas. She stood there with the clear glasses in her hands, the dust not having time to gather on them since she had moved there in August, and Ken in the next room, asking her when she was coming in to watch "White Christmas" with him. She should have poured the soda into the glasses, added a few ice cubes, and been on her way. But Sarah couldn't do it. She looked at the glasses again, then back at the open doorway where she could see the top of Ken's head with the big Tupperware bowl of popcorn in his lap, and she put the glasses back in the cabinet. Instead she pulled out some others, some her mother had given her, castoffs from somewhere in the McCall family's life.

Sarah wondered: was she scared to use the glasses because they represented Jenna's hopefulness at the time? And with Jenna gone, had she misplaced that same hopefulness in her life?

She still hadn't used them. Sarah shut the cabinet and left the kitchen. She could dust them another day. It wasn't like the dust was going anywhere anyway. A few more particles weren't going to make a difference.

*****

Tracing the road to Jenna's suicide had been difficult. It was like drawing a map without having any sense of the direction or where she was trying to go. Actually, she knew where she was going. The destination was Jenna's suicide. It was where Sarah started that she couldn't pinpoint.

But to tell the story like that was one-sided. There was a pained shadow to Jenna although few knew about it. Few saw it. Sarah knew it well. For as much as Jenna was Sarah's biggest supporter in her life, Jenna couldn't do the same for herself. And no matter how much they all supported her, she seemed to not love herself. It almost was as if something had been shut off inside her. No, maybe it had never been turned on. Sarah for so long had constantly reached back in her life and examined Jenna's life, at least everything she knew about it. She knew there were pieces she didn't know, that she would never know.

Sarah wondered if that's why she didn't get married. She was too busy trying to figure out Jenna's life and death, hoping it would make sense to her, that she didn't have time to devote to the nurturing that a relationship, such as marriage, that creating a family, deserved.

Was it too late? Was it important anymore? When she went to the grocery store and watched the couples shopping together, something she imagined people did together when their relationship was still new, when they still were discovering each other. They spent what looked like hours pouring over the entire cereal aisle as if they were planning their lives around which cereal would fit their routine best.

Then there were the women she saw without the husband but with the babies and the bigger kids. Life had changed by then. Had this all happened when Sarah was figuring out what it all meant? She watched her friends go through the changes in their marriages. The development from a couple to a family, sometimes with a dog before a baby.

The result of this for Sarah was that she had opted not to play by society's rules. Or were they the rules of life? But Jenna had ended her life. They had been taught, from birth, that this wasn't something they were supposed to do. No, not allowed to do. That would suspend someone to a lifetime of purgatory. Or was it hell? Sarah didn't know. She didn't remember most of what they taught in CCD. She knew just enough to pass whatever test it was and sail onto the next grade. It all got lost with everything else from elementary school and junior high as if it was muddled together in one pond. And since she never fished it out because she didn't need it, she forgot it all.

Had Jenna lived, it all would have been different. She and Jenna would have had the bakery. She knew they both would have married. How could she know? She realized people might ask. It didn't matter. She believed they both would. She believed that a lifetime of happiness was around the corner for both of them. The bakery, marriage, homes, children, baseball, cookies. What else could they have asked for?

Sometimes, though, she did wonder. Maybe that was the beginning of a long difficult road for Jenna. Did Jenna know something they didn't? Did Jenna sense an illness, one in her mind, coming on that scared her? She already was scared of so much but maybe this was what she was truly scared of. Herself.

It was with Jenna that Sarah always found their Christmas presents. Jenna was just about six when it started, Sarah was eight. They were in their mom's closet when they stumbled on bags from a local toy store. At first they didn't realize they had struck gold. Sarah could still remember that she thought the bags were from something else. But when she opened one, she saw the new Barbie doll she'd asked Santa Claus to bring her. And there was the Barbie bathroom she asked for as well. All the presents they wanted, right there in the closet.

"Doesn't Santa bring all these?" Jenna had asked, looking a little baffled.

It hadn't occurred to Sarah that her sister's dream of Santa was dashed.

"Oh Jenna, you know that Santa can't carry all these in his sleigh," she reminded her. "Silly. Mom and Dad are just helping him out."

Sarah already had been doubting that Santa existed by then but she realized she didn't want to dash her sister's hope about him. Probably the first time she sought to protect her sister.

And now she wondered why she couldn't protect Jenna from ending her life. She continued to wonder why Jenna never called her, never reached out to her. Or wondered if maybe she missed it.

They wouldn't always find the Christmas presents after that. They never were brave enough to ask their mother if she was onto them and moved them around. Or if she just did it because she couldn't remember where she had placed them the year before.

*****

There was a downpour the day after Jenna died. Sarah sat in the back of the dark chapel at the cemetery, Matt next to her. Waking up that morning, at first it didn't feel like it happened. She thought maybe Jenna was in her bed like any other morning before school. But then why would Sarah be at home? Sarah rolled herself out of bed and walked down the hall to Jenna's bedroom.

When she walked in, she instantly knew she was wrong. The cord she used was still on the floor. Sarah's mood fell back into the pool of sadness. She picked up the cord and threw it in the garbage can filled with papers and tissues. At first she sat on the bed, then realizing she was cold, she pulled the comforter back and climbed under it. How many times had they climbed into each other's beds at night, in the morning, or various other times of day? Sometimes it was because one was sad, other times because they were bored. The thought of it never happening again made Sarah cry.

Now she sat in the chapel of the cemetery where they had just picked a plot for Jenna. Her body would rest under what would be a shady tree in the summer. Now it just looked barren and sad, the rain drenching everything.

"These aren't even April showers," her mother sighed from the front seat.

"February showers," her father muttered as he drove.

Her parents kneeled in the first row of the chapel now. And when Sarah looked up, she could see her father shaking under his coat. She glanced at Matt, as if he might understand the disbelief, and then back at her dad. For the first time in her life, she saw her father crying. And not just his eyes welling up with tears but the uncontrollable shaking that comes with tears of sadness and pain.

Frank McCall always was the epitome of strength. Sarah counted on her father to be a rock for the family even when he angered her as she grew up and she thought he was unreasonable. Her mother nurtured all of them, her father held them up. Sarah thought all families were like that. It wasn't perfect, she knew, but it worked for them. And it seemed to work better than the roles other families played.

But she started to think that, even in twenty-four hours, Jenna's death had broken him in a way she never could have expected or understood. In time she would sense his fear of failure that he hadn't rescued Jenna from her pain or that he hadn't shielded her with his strength. He had failed to hold Jenna up.

Her mother reached for her father's hand, the right one, the one that held his sobbing face, and they grasped hold of each other in a way that Sarah never saw before. Maybe it was a way she reached for him each night after they shut the door of their bedroom. Somehow he would have to hold her up and she would have to nurture him. But maybe now the rules had changed. The journey was different and maybe that meant the roles would reverse.

They sat there for what felt like an eternity. Sarah wondered if they were praying to God. Asking for what? That she be let into Heaven? Sarah shook her head. Even if Jenna had hung herself, surely God would let Jenna into Heaven. If he didn't, Sarah wanted to go wherever her sister was.

She wished that Matt would speak to her. He looked straight ahead as if he couldn't feel anything. She wondered if she pricked him, would he react? It was just her and Matt. It felt disappointing.

Matt. Sarah's big brother. Once Sarah and Jenna's big brother. But really now, just Matt. He thought Sarah and Jenna were annoying. That didn't change as they got older either. He was stoic on this day just like he was any other day that Sarah remembered him in her life.

*****

There were many times when Sarah found herself reaching for the phone, wanting to call her sister and tell her things. Not just about boys, or men, but about life. When she heard U2 had a new cd, when she got her first teaching job, when one of her students came in acting just like Jenna, bouncing around the room in purple, she wanted to call and tell her sister all about it.

How could Jenna take that away from them? Sarah always wondered. Didn't she want to continue sharing through life? That was the plan anyway. Why did she alter it? She wished her sister had left her a note, something to tell her what to do without her and why she left. In many ways it felt as if Jenna walked out the door one day without any answers for her family or anyone else. And the only answer to herself was to end her life that afternoon.

Several times Sarah found herself dialing her parents' house, hoping to catch Jenna to tell her something. And more than one time her father answered the phone, putting Sarah in an odd place.

"I was calling for Jenna," she would say, sheepishly.

"It's okay," Frank McCall would tell his daughter, "I've called up the stairs more than once to ask her something or to call her to dinner." She could hear the quiver in his voice. She knew he fought the tears. He had just told her the week before that they all needed to go on. It had been a year, they all needed to go on. But it was clear he understood that wasn't possible. There was still unfinished business. Stuff they wouldn't ever understand. Jenna took it all with her.

"I know, Dad," Sarah would say quietly, not wanting to interrupt his pain.

She began to feel the lessons from Jenna's death. It only had been a year but she sensed she was becoming someone different. And it wasn't that she didn't like this person she was becoming; she felt as though she wasn't sure who this person was. Whether she liked her or not was still up in the air.

Sarah found herself, although annoyed a lot of the time because grief was taxing, developing into a much more compassionate person. She found herself more tearful during movies or when listening to friends discuss breakups or the jobs they applied for and didn't get. She wanted to hug people for the first time in her life. She wanted to hold them and tell them they would be okay. It forced her to forget her own pain. Maybe it was Jenna coming out of her. Jenna loved almost everyone and everything. Whatever it was, she felt herself changing.

And that was another reason she knew it would never last with Ken. She wasn't sure who she would be when she finally came out of her grief. She wasn't sure if it meant that one day she would exit with a diploma that she had made it. Surely it wasn't that simple. Maybe she would wake up one day and know that she had processed as far as she could.

What Sarah mostly hoped was that she wouldn't feel this bad forever. She relied on Kayla as her hope that she would eventually be okay. Kayla had been thirteen, still in adolescence when her father died. Sarah was older, she knew how to maneuver life at least a little better than a thirteen year old. At least she hoped she did.

"It's not perfect but I'm okay," Kayla would say, her eyes watering a little. "I'll always miss him but I'm going to be okay."

Sarah was glad to leave KU behind. She was ready to move into the next phase of her life. She loved her time there but felt a need to move on, to go do something new, to leave behind the place of her intense grief. But she would miss Kayla. And after graduation if someone had asked her what taught her the biggest lessons at KU, she would have said that Kayla inspired her to believe that there was hope that she, too, would be okay.

CHAPTER 18

Jenna wasn't the easiest person to get along with. Sarah realized most people didn't know that. They thought she was a bubbly, happy girl. She was definitely a bubbly, happy girl. But she could be mean and grouchy all the same. And bitchy. Sarah never could have admitted before Jenna died that Jenna, too, was bitchy, but after her death she realized that sometimes two sisters, only a few years apart, living under the same roof, wasn't always a good idea.

Sarah sometimes thought about this as she stood in the hall between classes, watching the students file past her, often ignoring her (unless they were her students or on her tennis team). She watched the range of emotions: the giggly girls laughing with their friends, the girls glaring at a friend or a boyfriend, and the girls who kept to themselves. Her memory of Jenna had been of a giggly girl in the hall with her friends. But after she'd gone to college, she wasn't sure if that changed since Sarah was no longer in the same place as her sister.

She tried to get into the halls between at least one passing period during each day. It broke up the monotony of her never-ending grading. She was happy she'd been teaching long enough that she only had to fine tune her lesson plans, not create complete new ones like those first years of settling into the routine.

"Hey," Mark greeted her, almost missing her as he walked quickly by, usually with a paper in one hand and a pen in the other. "I got so used to you in your classroom that I forget what you look like outside of it."

Sarah laughed. "Contrary to popular belief, I do leave my classroom and the tennis court sometimes."

They talked for a few minutes before the warning bell rang, sending the kids scattering and them to their respective classrooms. Sarah found her thoughts lingering on Jenna more this year than in recent prior years. She would roll her pen across the calendar on her desk, watching her students take an essay test, remembering what life had been like before Jenna died. And after Jenna's suicide.

~ Sisters: The Karma Twist ~

*****

She and Jenna fought over everything from hairspray to the time each of their parents spent with them. One time Frank McCall, in a fit of annoyance at them, called out (his fists clenched at his side), "Is there anything you two don't fight about?!" Sarah and Jenna had been arguing over whose sweatshirt it was that had been left in the kitchen.

They stood there, the sweatshirt held in each of their hands as if they were going to play tug-o-war with it, and looked at each other. Then they started laughing. Eventually Sarah laughed so hard that she doubled over to hold her stomach, leaving Jenna with the sweatshirt in her hand. She then whacked her sister in the head with it.

Their father walked away, at least looking happy that instead of screaming he had uncontrollable laughter under his roof.

It didn't always end so peacefully. Arlene McCall sometimes told the girls stories about how they used to throw their toys at each other and how it worried her as the toys got larger and the girls got stronger. Matt had basically been an only child since he was off at school when Sarah came along. She hadn't had to break up any fights unless it was between him and one of the neighborhood boys over a baseball game. And usually then she was too late, most of the fight having ensued by the time she looked out her living room window and saw what was going on, both boys sporting bloody noses.

Once Sarah nailed Jenna in the forehead with a toy that left a red welt and Jenna crying to their mother. "It wasn't funny then," Arlene McCall would laugh over the years, her eyes watering at the thought of the memory, "but seeing you two now, I'm glad you got the throwing stage out early and that you advanced to verbal fighting only. I'd hate to get between you two now."

*****

What was left of Jenna's life went to Sarah when her parents moved. Matt waved a hand when Sarah pointed to the boxes left in Jenna's old room. "I don't want them," he said, shaking his head and walking out of the room. Sarah wasn't sure why she kept longing to talk to him. She knew he didn't have the same memories as her. She told Barbara that she didn't want to lose all of her sibling memories. Her parents didn't want Jenna's things either. "We won't have room in the new condo in Florida," they insisted.

Sarah packed the four boxes that represented Jenna's life and stored them in a closet in her apartment until she bought her house several years later. They were tucked into a corner of the closet of her guest room, a place she didn't often go. But one afternoon she walked in there looking for something, that "something" she wouldn't remember later, and found herself unable to stay out of the boxes.

Whatever was in those boxes was what Sarah had opted to save. Her parents gave her free reign to decide what was left of Jenna's life. Her yearbooks, her *Little House on the Prairie* books that she read until they became dog-eared, several of her favorite shirts, her big purple fuzzy slippers, and countless other items that Sarah thought would be how she remembered her sister.

The fourth box was the largest and held some of their childhood toys. Mostly the Barbie dolls. Sarah pulled each one out of the box as if they were long-lost friends. She touched their hair, remembered their names, and looked for their favorite outfits, all the while recalling all the good times she and Jenna had playing with them. They all had lives, they were perfect, they had jobs– no, they had careers, and they had families. There was never a worry about money or illness or anything else. Unless they created it.

If only life had been that easy. Sometimes Sarah wondered if maybe Jenna had the right idea, maybe it was better to check out early before it got difficult. She watched Barbara and her husband struggle to raise their kids and maintain a relationship together. And Julie giving up her career for a baby. And then Sarah herself feeling like she didn't have much of a family since her sister had died. Maybe the dolls had it right. Let someone else create your life for you, Sarah thought, holding her favorite one, the matriarch of her doll family, in her 1970s pink evening gown.

"I wish you were here," she mumbled to Jenna under her breath. As she felt the tears come, she put the dolls away, packed the boxes back into the closet, and left the room without getting what she walked in there for.

Thinking about Jenna always distracted her. Sometimes she thought she was losing her memory. Walking into a room and forgetting why she was there wasn't unheard of for her. She did it often in the first year or so after Jenna died. She was thankful it ended before she started teaching although she had several students who reminded her a lot of Jenna. She would smile at them and wish somehow they were Jenna or that Jenna had sent them to her. She wished they had messages from her sister. She still wished life had been different.

*****

Few people knew that Sarah struggled with relationships as much as she did. Most people simply thought she was too busy teaching and coaching to have time for them. She did have the time. She knew she did. Instead, she used a lot of it to turn herself off to what she could have. It was hard to explain to anyone. It was different before Jenna died. She didn't fear relationships. She didn't fear letting anyone into her life. But after Jenna died, she felt such a loss of control that she vowed, unconsciously, she would never go there again. No one would ever have that control over her life to make her hurt that badly.

She'd had no boyfriend when Jenna died. She had too much school ahead of her and the goals with Jenna and the bakery. It could wait. But when Jenna died, it all changed. She still didn't know why she let Ken in. "A weak moment," she would joke to Barbara after it was over.

And Barbara would snort back, "A weak moment that lasted almost two years."

She was right. It made no sense. The worst of it was she felt that in the end she had wasted Ken's time. He deserved someone who wanted to be with him long term and she couldn't give it to him. She had tried in the beginning. She had thought maybe she could change her thinking, that she could let him in and maybe they could have the life of many of their friends. They attended countless weddings in those twenty months together. Her friends, his friends, and then their friends at Kansas. And each time the bride or groom would ask, "Are you two next?"

In the beginning, Ken would squeeze Sarah's hand and smile at her. "We'll see." There was no reason for him not to be hopeful at that time. She tried. Deep down she wasn't hopeful but she knew she tried. As the weddings passed them by, Ken stopped squeezing her hand and smiling when someone asked. Mostly, they both shuffled uncomfortably. It had become a sore subject for both of them.

When Sarah started teaching, it wasn't long before the football coach asked her for a date. Then the social studies teacher in the next hall. She liked them all. They were nice men. But it was easy to cut it short.

"You have football," she'd say, "and I have tennis. We have to wait until the offseason." He was in the process of a divorce anyway. It was better that they waited. The social studies teacher was a little harder to put off. He was persistent, constantly stopping by her classroom to talk. "I'm sorry," she finally said, "I really like you but I need to focus on my work right now."

"How do you do it?" the boys tennis coach, an older man named Steve, would ask her later when they had a meeting to discuss the resurfacing of the tennis courts the next summer.

"How do I do what?" she asked, sitting in Steve's math classroom.

"Everyone seems to think that since we both coach tennis, I know a lot about you." Sarah laughed. They hardly saw each other since their teams played in separate seasons. "They keep asking if you're single and if they know you're single, they want to know why you don't seem to date. Please tell me that you have a boyfriend in England or something so I can make them go away."

Sarah laughed. She had to laugh because she couldn't tell him the truth. Then she shrugged her shoulders. "It just hasn't worked out."

"Then maybe you should go on a date with me and I'll make something up about us," he suggested.

Sarah knew he was kidding and her stomach began to hurt as she laughed harder. "I'm sure your wife would be happy about that," she reminded him.

"That I went out with someone half my age?"

Part of her wished she could tell him the truth. No one at the school knew about her sister. She wasn't sure if that was good or bad but it was what she felt she had to do to function. She was in her first year of teaching. She had tennis, she had lesson plans. She didn't get why that wasn't enough to put these men off from asking her on dates. Eventually they would stop asking. Baseball coach Mark was new. He didn't know her. He didn't know her history. And if he had asked anyone about it, either he hadn't listened or he didn't care. He wanted to ask her out anyway.

Those were some of the main times when Sarah wanted to reach out to Jenna, to call her and talk to her. Jenna's encouragement would be enough to keep her going. Any fears that Sarah had would dissipate when she talked to Jenna. "Go for it. You always tell me you have nothing to lose, right?" Jenna would say.

And she was right. Sarah always did tell Jenna that.

Several times Sarah had been tempted to drive to Cedarville, to drive to the cemetery to "see" Jenna. She felt that if she sat by the grave, if she went where Jenna's body was, then maybe Jenna would come to her. Maybe she would sense something from Jenna that would help her. She knew she was panicking and being irrational. She would call Barbara instead.

"I just wish I could talk to her," she would cry. "It's not that I don't want to talk to you. I miss her though."

"Of course you do," Barbara would say. Sarah would picture Barbara, rubbing her growing belly at the time, her first baby due in several months. She knew their lives were on different paths but she also knew she needed to cling to the friends she had. Without Jenna, who else was going to help her?

"Sarah," Barbara said gently one day. Sarah sensed a change in her friend in her pregnancy, just as she had sensed a change in herself since Jenna died. They both had different levels of understanding although they were reaching them in very unique ways. "I know you're scared because she's not here. But I hope that one day you will let someone in. I hope one day you'll let someone love you the way you deserve to be loved. Don't close yourself off forever."

She couldn't answer. Sarah sat on the other end of the phone, unable to move or to speak. Deep inside, somewhere that she couldn't reach, she knew that Barbara was right. How would she get there though? Sarah couldn't answer that. How would she free herself from her own fears?

*****

There were good times with Ken. Sometimes Sarah had to remind herself of them because she got so lost in how difficult it became to sustain a relationship with him. She'd had a few boyfriends in high school but nothing more than hanging out at each other's houses on Friday nights or going to school dances. Those were the relationships she shared with Jenna and Jenna with her as they made their way through high school,

Sarah had a feeling more boys liked Jenna than Jenna told her about. By the time Sarah left for college, she knew Jenna, as a senior, could take care of herself, but she never told her sister that she worried Jenna wasn't giving any of them a chance. She could sense a bit of fear on Jenna's part but she never could quite place what it was.

She and Ken met in an exercise class on campus. They were both graduate students, although in different departments, she in the English department and he in the athletic department where he thought one day he might be a college basketball coach. It wasn't baseball, Sarah had reasoned with herself, but it was probably better that way. The focus on school and Ken took it off Jenna and Sarah found that she enjoyed going to the games and waiting for Ken afterward to tell her what really happened on the floor.

What she didn't anticipate was the closeness that would develop between them. Often he would stay the night at her apartment, making his way back to his place when the sun began to rise or she left for class. One morning when he stood at the coffee maker in his shorts and t-shirt trying to decide if he should add more coffee grounds to jolt the caffeine after a late game, Sarah smiled when she walked by. All sense of routine had disappeared when Jenna had died. Ken brought her that back. It wasn't the same as before, Sarah knew it would never be the same as before, but she was grateful for it.

At least for a while.

One morning though, she woke up in a funk. She'd had a dream that Jenna was there. She kept saying, "I haven't died, I'm still with you. I'm still here." She and Sarah stood in Jenna's bedroom and Jenna was mad that they had cleaned out all her stuff and their parents were moving. "How could you get rid of my life?" she repeatedly asked.

Sarah's eyes bolted open when her alarm buzzed her awake. She turned her head to see Ken snoozing quietly beside her. And then she remembered it wasn't true. Jenna wasn't still alive. They hadn't messed up by "throwing out" her life as she said in the dream. She was gone. There was no need for all the "things" she was angry were missing.

For just a little while, although Jenna had been angry in the dream, Sarah felt a sense of calm that her sister was still there. She was alive. That's all that mattered. But now as she pushed herself out of bed, that calm dissipated into sadness that Jenna really wasn't still alive. Ken wasn't due to get up until she was ready to leave to teach her 10:00 class. Trying not to disturb him, she held off crying until she got into the shower.

The water was hot. Too hot. She knew it, too. But Sarah didn't have the energy to turn the faucet toward the blue cool side. She could barely get shampoo in her hair, her legs shaved, and her body washed. She only wanted to stand there and let the water roll over her like the sadness that she felt. Finally, she sat down in the shower, letting her body rest, even though it should have been ready for the day. Somehow she had to turn the water off and at least get wrapped in a towel. Somehow.

That somehow came from time. Sarah couldn't think of anything that might give her the motivation to leave the shower other than the fact that her students would be waiting for her at 10:00. They wouldn't be happy to be there, nor would she, but they would be waiting.

She made her way across the hall to the bedroom. She could hear Ken, up earlier than usual, in the kitchen making the coffee. She didn't want him to see her in tears. Sarah, green bath towel still wrapped around her body and a matching green one wrapped around her hair, slipped back into her side of the bed, finding comfort in the rumpled sheets and bedding. She wasn't crying now but she felt worn out and wished it were the end of the day.

"Hey, why are you back in bed? Are you okay?" Ken asked, walking in with his mug of coffee. He walked over to Sarah's side of the bed. "You look a little green. Or pale. Or something."

Sarah wanted to tell him that she had the flu or even that she had food poisoning. She knew that would send him away which was part of her plan. But that also was easier than admitting she was sad.

Ken knew her too well though and she realized she would never get away with any of it. "I had a bad dream," she finally croaked. He sat down on the side of the bed and took her hand.

"Then why didn't you wake me up?"

She shrugged her shoulders, knowing she didn't have an answer for that. "I just thought I had to get up and get the day going. But I feel like shit now."

Ken kissed her forehead. "Then stay in bed."

"Yeah, right," Sarah said, looking at the clock, the very clock with the time looming nearer that her students waited. "It's 8:30 and I have class in ninety minutes. You know that."

"Then tell me about your dream," he said, holding her hand, the cup of coffee still in the other one.

Sarah found she couldn't speak. One of the few times in her life she couldn't croak out an answer. But Ken didn't go anywhere. He didn't ask for anything else. He just sat and waited. Sarah knew many women would love to have Ken. But she wished she had him under what she called "more normal circumstances." If suicide loss was so unique, then why did she have to experience it?

"It was about my sister," she said. It felt like five minutes had gone by.

Ken placed the coffee mug on the nightstand next to the clock with the looming time. "I know you have to leave," he whispered. "And I know you won't tell me about your sister. But maybe for twenty minutes you'll let me lay here with you."

Sarah wasn't going to say no. She pushed herself across the bed to make room for him behind her. He wrapped his arms around her, towel and all, and she let herself drift away. At least for twenty minutes. When she sat up to get up and dress for class he patted her arm, "Maybe now you have enough energy to get through the day."

Sarah smiled, giving him a kiss on the forehead.

Looking back, this made Sarah sad. It made her realize how much she did miss out on something really special. Ken had been willing to give her something that she knew, especially after hearing Kayla's stories and the ones she read about in the books where people divorced after suicide loss, yet she was too scared to take it. Too scared to let him in. Too scared because Jenna was too scared and she realized she let Jenna's suicide begin to dictate parts of her life.

Most people didn't know how fearful she was. The girls she coached thought she walked on water. When there wasn't a group of students, particularly boys, in her classroom outside the season, her girls usually gathered to do homework. "A safe haven," Sarah would joke to her friends. "I provide them a safe haven for some reason."

~ Sisters: The Karma Twist ~

When they weren't doing homework, they wanted to tell Sarah about their boyfriends, about how their parents drove them crazy, about how much they hated doing homework. But then the questions would turn to Sarah.

One day they were in Sarah's classroom while it snowed outside. The season had just ended and the girls couldn't let go of their time together. She encouraged them to find something to do in the winter months (none of them was interested in playing basketball, or even badminton, the two winter sports offered for girls, although a few would go out for track in the spring), yet they wanted to stay with Sarah after school. Sarah had given up grading papers. She knew the papers could wait. They would still be there later that evening or tomorrow. She'd had Jenna to bounce life off in high school. The least she could do was be there for her girls.

Suddenly, they all stared at each other and the bravest one to do anything, anything at all from singing out loud on the bus to asking a boy out on a date, Amy Graf blurted out, "Why aren't you married?"

Sarah sat back and in her chair, the one that tilted back enough to make her feel like she was important in the world, and smiled. What else could she do? The girls weren't being nosy. They were curious.

"We all think you're so pretty and we don't understand why you aren't married," Amy added.

Sarah sat forward again and doodled with her red pen on the big paper calendar that spread across the mid-section of her desk. What would she tell them? How would she get them to understand that life had changed much of her dreams from their age? She didn't want to burst their bubbles. She wanted them to be hopeful, to know that life was great, and they were meant to dream big.

"You know," she said, putting her pen down and sitting back again so she could look at the five girls, "I had big dreams when I was your age. I knew I could accomplish anything I wanted to. I knew that the world was my oyster."

"Then something changed?" Amy was the only one, as usual, brave enough to ask.

Sarah debated. Did she tell them. Did she not tell them. No one at the school knew. "My sister died," she finally said, looking up at them. The room filled with gasps and then went quiet.

"Like a long time ago?" Amy asked. Sarah knew Amy would ask all the questions. She wondered if the others would filter them through her via telepathy.

"When I was in college and she was in high school."

"Did she die in a car accident? Was she sick?"

They have no clue, Sarah thought. Their lives, while not perfect, she knew were far from perfect, but they had yet to be touched by a loss such as suicide. Sarah wished she were still one of them.

"No, she killed herself."

The gasp slithered through the room again. And then it went quiet. Just like before. Even Amy didn't have anything to ask.

"What happened?" Sheila Darnell's voice came from the back of the room.

"The best we know, she had a lot of fear that maybe she was getting sick, mentally sick, and it scared her."

"Is that why you always harp on us at the beginning of the season to make sure we talk to you or someone else if we're having any problems?" Marcy Brown asked.

Sarah smiled. "And you were apparently listening."

Marcy smiled back. "I'm always listening. But I've heard you say it for three years now."

"What did you do?" Amy looked as if for the first time she could speak. "I can't imagine if my sister died. I can't imagine."

"None of us can imagine it," Sarah told her, putting her hands in her lap. She felt a warmness in the room with the girls although part of her felt a little cold. She wished she had a blanket to wrap around herself. Maybe it wasn't so much that she was cold but rather that she wanted some comfort. She thought she needed comfort to talk to the girls. It wouldn't work that way though. She was on her own to do this. "But when it happens you have to deal with it, cope with it."

"How old was she?" Sheila moved in closer and so did Doreen Shipley who was in the back of the room with Sheila.

"She was seventeen, a senior."

"And you?"

"I was three years ahead of her. I was a junior in college when it happened." And slowly the details emerged. Sarah shared as openly as she could with the girls about what happened to Jenna and how it had altered her life. The girls didn't move. She didn't share about baseball or the bakery. "I didn't plan to become a teacher," was all she said and they didn't question it.

"If your sister hadn't died, where do you think you might be?" Amy asked, looking up at the clock. It was nearing 5:00 and Sarah knew they would be going home, just where she needed to go to see Mairzy.

This was an easy question but she wasn't sure the answer was so easy. "You think your life is going to be one thing. You spend so much of life just dreaming about where you want to be and who you want to be with. Sometimes you wake up and realize that you never pursued that. My life would have been very different if Jenna hadn't died. I know that. But I'm not sure that I could tell you now who I might have been. Five years ago I would have given you a different answer. All I can say is treasure each day you have with everyone."

"And we do with you!" Sheila reminded Sarah.

They got up to leave and Sarah followed them out, shutting the locked classroom door behind her. She could see the snow sticking on the street and thought it would take her a little longer to get home. But just like she understood now that it was okay that she had shared with the girls, she also knew the drive home would be okay.

CHAPTER 19

The summer after Jenna died, Sarah happened to run into Jenna's best friend at the drugstore in town. Sarah didn't see Tami at first. She was too busy trying to pick a conditioner for her dried out hair.

"Hey," Tami said, touching Sarah's arm.

"Hey," Sarah said, shaking herself out of thoughts about split ends. "How are you? Are you excited for college?"

"I'm okay. How are you?" Tami looked a little unsettled at first. Then she blurted out, "It's weird to have graduated without her. She was supposed to be with us, you know." Tami shuffled her feet where she stood. "I really wanted to talk to you, to talk to your mom. But I've been too afraid to call."

"Why?" Sarah asked. "We've wanted to talk to you but you know I just got back."

"I'm not sure what to say. And I'm afraid I'll start crying." She stopped because she was crying. "See? I'm crying. I can't stop crying when I think about her. I was afraid I would make your mom cry if I cried."

"Oh Tami, you know how much Mom wants to see you."

Sarah knew people milled around them. She felt them as if they were in the periphery of her vision. But she couldn't sense more than that because Tami's pain, and her own, took up the immediate vicinity.

"Come over. Come over and we'll talk."

Tami was over that evening, right after dinner. Arlene McCall hugged the girl who had spent many nights at their house. Frank McCall hid. Sarah saw him briefly. He took off his glasses to wipe tears from his eyes. Sarah began to wonder if they all would ever stop crying. Just seeing tears from her dad made her own tearful waterfall start. Sarah wasn't sure that she felt sad at the moment about Jenna being gone so much as she felt sad about everyone else crying and feeling that much pain.

"I was wondering if there were a few things of hers that I could have?" Tami asked Sarah's mother. "I had a t-shirt I bought her from Illinois when I went for my visit and there's a sweatshirt she got one day when we were shopping."

Arlene nodded and took Tami's hand. Together they walked upstairs to Jenna's room, Sarah following. At that point it was still just as she left it, sans a few things that had been removed or the bed being made. All Jenna's laundry that had been in the laundry room the day she died now sat in piles on her dresser as if she might need it.

"What was I supposed to do with it?" Sarah's mother had asked Sarah as if Sarah could help her. "I couldn't just leave it in the hamper forever. We'll have to do something with it eventually."

Sarah placed her palm on the pile of t-shirts, watching Tami walk around the room. "It still doesn't seem real," she finally said. "She was just here."

Arlene looked for the sweatshirt that Tami had asked for. Sarah still didn't feel comfortable going through her sister's things. It reminded her of when they were younger and Jenna had rifled through her stuff. She'd been so angry. She had such a sense of disrespect now if she did it. She couldn't put two and two together that Jenna would no longer need any of those things.

Tami ran her fingers across notebooks and books on the desk, across the dresser. She stared into the open closet, Jenna's formal dresses still hanging as if they might see use again.

By then, Sarah's mother had left the room. Sarah sat down on the bed, crossing her legs in front of her, just as she had done a million times before with Jenna in the room.

Tami sat next to her on the bed, pulling her hair tie out of her long blonde hair and reaching back to redo it. Sarah didn't think it looked any different. But she understood. Tami looked to control something. She couldn't control that her friend was gone. But she could control the state of her hair.

"I wish I had known how much pain she was in," Tami said sadly, staring at Jenna's purple furry slippers on the floor.

~ Sisters: The Karma Twist ~

"Me, too," Sarah said, looking glumly at the same slippers.

"Can I tell you something?" Tami finally asked after what felt like five minutes of silence.

Sarah looked up at Tami.

"I think something was happening. I don't know how to describe it. And I don't think she knew what it was. But she was scared."

Sarah nodded her head, getting off the bed and retrieving the journals from Jenna's desk drawer. "Look at this," she said showing Tami what she had found. "Something was happening to her."

"Did you show this to your parents?" Tami asked, reading through the pages. When she teared up again, Sarah went to the bathroom and retrieved a box of tissues.

Sarah shook her head. "I know I should but I'm afraid to. It will devastate them. I don't know if it was depression or if it was the onset of some mental illness but something was very wrong."

"Maybe it wasn't even that," Tami said, "maybe she was physically sick in some way. I had a cousin once who did all these weird things and it turned out he had a tumor in his brain."

"I don't know," Sarah said, sadly, focusing on the slippers. "I just wish she had reached out to someone, anyone, for help."

That night, Sarah finally found the courage to show her parents the journals. Neither one had been through Jenna's things. It was easier for them not to. And she also knew that the unsaid expectation was that she would be the one to clean out Jenna's room.

She brought the journals to them in the family room where they were into their nightly television routine. Sarah opened to the pages where Jenna wrote about the blackness she couldn't see beyond, where she wrote about the fear that overcame her. Then she handed a journal to each of them. "I found these a few weeks ago. I think something else was going on."

As Arlene McCall read, she placed her hand over her mouth, covering it as if she might vomit on the pages. But then she began to let out tiny shrieks. Sarah knew it was her pain. Frank McCall took off his glasses again, wiping his eyes on his shirtsleeve.

"I think she was sick. I don't know if it was mental illness or depression but something else was going on."

"Why didn't she ask us for help?" Arlene kept crying over and over again. "We could have helped her."

"I don't think she knew how," Sarah said, crying because her parents were crying.

She knew she had devastated her parents. She wasn't sure that this information was helpful. Maybe it made it worse for them. Maybe she should have kept it to herself. Worse, she felt unsettled herself. It almost felt as if it created more questions rather than fewer. And as their relationship began to deteriorate, part of her always would wonder if it was because of what she shared with them.

*****

There were countless stories of people who experienced signs of their loved ones after they died. They ranged from seeing the person's face in a crowd to conversations with them in dreams at night. Sarah heard them at the support group she attended, and she read about them in books (especially the ones her mother gave her to read). And then there were the "Pennies from Heaven" stories she read about in "Dear Abby" in the newspaper. But Sarah had never felt Jenna's presence. She longed to hear her sister flying down the stairs at their parents house once again, she wished she could hear her laugh, but most of all she just wanted to know she was Jenna.

It was silly, she knew it was silly. Surely Jenna was with her. But this was part of what nagged at her about faith and religion: trusting the unseen. Sarah wanted some concrete proof, she wanted Jenna to come to her and tell her she was okay. Other people had these experiences? Why couldn't she? Why wouldn't her sister come to her and tell her she was okay, she wasn't in hell or purgatory or wherever else the church might say she was. Whatever had been hurting her, whatever it was she didn't believe she could face was gone. It had been torn away once she crossed over into what Sarah always thought of as Jenna's new life. The life where she was free of worry, pain, and most of all, fear.

The tennis courts at Mill West, the school where Sarah taught, were on the east side of the campus next to the rest of the playing fields. There wasn't much to shield them from wind although some days they were lucky and the wind stayed low enough that no one complained that the person on the other side was getting the better end of the deal. Conference teams dreaded dual matches played on the Mill West courts. Sarah taught her girls to use it to their advantage, but that didn't mean they were quiet about it. They complained endlessly, especially as the season wore on and the fall weather turned toward winter.

One afternoon Sarah hit balls to her top singles player, Marla Davenport, on a sunless, windless day. It was just warm enough that everyone was comfortable in tennis skirts. Marla took a break to get a drink and Sarah stood, a ball in hand, bouncing it up and down while she waited.

As she looked up, she felt something though. It was a blast of air. Warm air. She looked around wondering what could have caused it?

"Coach! What's with the strange look?" Marla called across the court.

Sarah shook her head unable to speak at first. Then she looked up at Marla. "Did you feel that?"

"Feel what?" Marla asked, throwing her racket up in the air and catching it. "All I can feel is how sore I'll be tonight after hitting all these balls."

Sarah stood still. It was Jenna. It had to have been Jenna. Why else would she have felt a blast of warm air on a fall day?

Getting ready to hit balls at Marla again, Sarah softly whispered, "Thank you," to her sister. She heard somewhere that if you say thank you, they will continue to visit you.

But it would be some time before she had a sense of Jenna again.

CHAPTER 20

Sarah worked part time at a dental office as she had each summer before Jenna's death. Sometimes Sarah would catch her mother standing in the doorway of Jenna's room, her back to Sarah who was in the hall. She never interrupted her mother's thoughts. She didn't think she could understand what she was going through. Nor could her mother understand what Sarah was experiencing. And so they didn't speak of their grief.

The routine of the McCall family that summer consisted of the same routine it had every summer when everyone was working, coming and going. Dinner was on the table at six. They discussed their days. They talked about the weather. They talked about what was needed at the grocery store. But they didn't talk about what happened to Jenna.

They didn't talk about Jenna because they denied her existence. Sarah knew this. Instead, everyone was hurting so much they didn't know how to reach out for each other. They had once been a fairly open family. Sarah remembered her mother once sitting her and Jenna down to discuss birth control if they chose to be sexually active. Both girls were embarrassed watching their mother explain what they didn't want to hear from her.

"I don't want you to ever be in a situation where you can't come to me," their mother had said to them.

Now Sarah watched her across the dinner table, cutting her chicken. Sarah knew she had to feel like she failed somewhere. She'd tried hard to make sure her daughters would go to her for help. And when one really needed help– she didn't.

Her father took a bite of his salad. She knew he wondered where he, too, had gone wrong. They all wondered what they did wrong. Or what they missed. But instead of talking about it, everyone acted as if it was okay. They could all go on as long as they didn't mention Jenna because that meant picking at wounds that were supposed to be healing. But Sarah wondered if they really were healing. If they all felt that much pain, didn't that mean they weren't healing?

*****

The thought was so embarrassing that Sarah didn't want to admit to anyone, especially herself, that she had had it. But if it was hers, maybe she should take ownership for it, she wondered. Why did everything seem easier when Jenna was alive? Sarah couldn't help but think she was jaded, that the way she remembered things weren't really as they were. And Jenna wasn't there to whack her on the back and say, "Duh! You just have selective memory." No one had a better memory than Jenna.

How many times did Sarah drive to the cemetery, needing someone to talk to, no, needing Jenna to talk to. And Jenna wasn't there but the cemetery was the one place she could go and feel somewhat of her sister's presence. She would sit on the grave, jokingly talking to Jenna as if she was there, reminding her that she sat on top of her. The grass was always itchy. She knew her mother was never happy with the way the flowers looked. Her father complained they had no clue how to take care of the grass. He didn't get it because it was a cemetery and that's what cemetery workers did. And someone always left something in that first year from rocks to flowers that had long died before Sarah arrived at the grave.

Sometimes people would be visiting other graves. This wasn't a place where you waved to people and started conversations with them. So Sarah sat there by herself and talked to her sister. It was as if Jenna had zonked out on her on a Saturday night after a long swim meet while Sarah was wide awake and not eager to go to sleep.

"I don't know why we bothered to let you two have your own rooms," their mother often joked in the mornings when she found them both in one bed or the other.

Usually it was about boys. She missed talking to Jenna about boys. They didn't share everything although there really wasn't time for everything. There was too much ahead that they would never share. And Jenna would never experience.

"Maybe I'm just an idiot," Sarah would sigh, picking at the grass in front of Jenna's headstone. Sometimes she ran her fingers across the drilled lettering of Jenna's name as if that would help make it more real that her sister was gone. And help Sarah feel alive. "I can't do this boy thing without you so maybe I shouldn't do it at all."

That was the thought, the one she didn't want anyone to know about. And here she had just about succeeded in not getting involved with any men since Jenna died. Except for Ken. Maybe she got involved with Ken because she was too far from home to visit Jenna at the cemetery. She was too far away from being reminded why she shouldn't have accepted that first date. And the second date. But she was home for Christmas, right before New Year's, when Ken started to talk marriage. And that's when Sarah ran the other way. Moving back to Chicago made that easy. She didn't apply for any of the open jobs in Kansas City that Ken told her about or handed her applications for. Instead, she went home.

And now she had Mark, the baseball coach, on her hands. Or did she? Dinner finished, the dishes done, Sarah sat at her dining room table attempting to finish grading papers. But the thought of Mark made her drop her head to the table on top of Veronica Mueller's discussion of *The Old Man and the Sea*. How will I win this battle? Sarah asked herself, giving up and turning out the light for the night.

CHAPTER 21

Ten, Sarah thought. There is such significance to the number ten. She kept thinking of more instances why it was an important number. Not just in tennis but in life. Big parties for tenth wedding anniversaries. Turning ten years old means you've entered into double digits (sounds exciting until you realize that there's no turning back once you get there). Ten dozen cookies.

As she made the cookies for the baseball team, she thought about ten years of cookie making on the day Jenna hanged herself in her closet in her bedroom. As Sarah creamed the butter, her thoughts kept turning back to Jenna and that morning she told their mom she was sick and wanted to stay home from school. Mom went to work. Dad went to work. And Jenna ended her life that afternoon for their mother to find her when she came home. And they still didn't understand why. Everyone said she was fine at school the day before. They never would completely get it. Jenna took those answers with her. They could only speculate with what they knew.

Sarah had talked to her a few days before. She seemed her usual happy self. But somewhere Sarah wondered if she had lost hope. She didn't get it though. They had their dream. It was the bakery that kept them going. When Sarah felt like she couldn't survive another chemistry class or another business class, Jenna cheered her on. Sarah fully expected to do the same for Jenna when she was in college. But she never got that far.

The towels she bought Jenna for a Christmas gift, the prep for dorm life, were still in Sarah's linen closet. She should use them, she knew. Ten years was a long time to let a set of green and purple towels sit unused. And now the colors looked dated. Sarah wondered what was she was saving them for? Jenna wasn't coming back. Why didn't she just use them?

Sarah added the sugar and wondered why so often people don't let others help them. Why do we truly listen when we're told to be independent? Why didn't Jenna reach out if she was scared of something? Sarah wiped her hair off her forehead. Jenna took all the answers with her. And Sarah knew part of her childhood was gone. She could only remember half of it now.

Making cookies that first year had been awful. Why did Sarah think she needed to do it? It had been a full year since she'd made any. It was her last trip home before Jenna died– the end of her winter vacation. They laughed like they usually did and talked about life, the things that were important to them then– boys, school, music, the upcoming start of baseball season.

But even baseball couldn't keep Jenna alive.

That first year Sarah cried as she dumped the butter out of the packaging into the bowl of the Kitchen Aid mixer her parents had bought her as a high school graduation gift. They had already bought Jenna's for her upcoming graduation. "I got a great deal on it," Arlene McCall had said, telling Sarah. "I bought it the day after Christmas." Now that mixer sat at her brother's house, used by Donna.

Each ingredient she poured into the bowl the first time she made cookies after Jenna died was one more ingredient that reminded her there would be no more cookies made with her sister. Their future was supposed to be made of cookies and pastries. They planned to start making kolacky when Sarah came home for summer break. And they were going to start marketing the cookies. They figured it would be a good way to get people amped up for their brand. No one knew that though. They wanted to wait until Sarah got home for the summer to announce it.

Instead, Sarah went home to a quiet house. One where Jenna wasn't chasing after her as she flew down the stairs to run out the front door and beat her to the car. After all, the last one there didn't get to drive to the store to get whatever they needed. And was a rotten egg.

But when Sarah had finished the cookies, the perfectly rounded shapes that she and Jenna had worked so hard to perfect over the years, she couldn't eat them. Alone in the apartment she shared with her roommates who were at class, she slipped them off the cooling rack and into the garbage can. She never told anyone she'd made a batch of cookies and thrown them out. It was wasteful. Surely someone would eat them, she knew. It was the symbolism behind the cookies though. And who could she explain that to at a university where few knew what she endured?

*****

~ Sisters: The Karma Twist ~

They suggested a support group. Sarah still couldn't remember who "they" was. Did it come from some relatives? There wasn't much information to search on the Internet in those days. And how did anyone find her a group for Kansas City? There wasn't one in Lawrence. She drove into Kansas City that first night, her hands shaking, not sure what she was going to find in the group.

When she walked into the room in the church, all she saw was a group of people just like her. People she might see at the grocery store. She wondered, was she disappointed? Did she expect them all to be pink or something?

"Hi, welcome to the Survivors of Suicide group," a kindly older woman with graying hair said while walking up to Sarah.

"Hi," was all Sarah could muster.

"Are you here for the group?" the woman asked, taking Sarah lightly by the arm and directing her to a banquet table filled with name tags, books, and a sign-in sheet. Sarah thought she must have looked overwhelmed because the woman began to slowly direct her. It was obvious she had done this a million times before.

"Who did you lose to suicide?" she asked. "My name is Margie Ross and I lost my son Kurt fifteen years ago."

"My sister," Sarah stammered. She didn't want to cry. She tried not to cry.

"It's okay if you cry," Margie said, waving at her. "Let it come. It must have been recent?"

Sarah couldn't help but focus on Margie's red sweater. She didn't know why. Maybe she needed something to stare at. "It was about eighteen months ago. I'm a graduate student at KU. I just moved here."

"Oh, a KU student," another women said, walking up to them. "We don't get too many. We know you need help as much as anyone else."

"There was no group in Lawrence," Sarah said, realizing it was a stupid thing to say. Surely they knew that.

Whatever they knew, Sarah realized they had some of the kindest faces she had ever seen. Mostly women made up the group although a few husbands hid in the corners. It was the women who wanted to talk, who wanted to take Sarah under their wings.

The men had placed the chairs into a big circle and the fifteen or so people each took one. Sarah had no idea what was next but Margie took the lead and they all followed.

It was hard to say Jenna's name out loud, to say that she had killed herself. But there also was a sense of comfort in this group of strangers. She knew they understood, that they knew what she was going through. And that she could say what she wanted.

She enjoyed the mothers who gave her hugs as if she were their daughter. Some of them had lost daughters, more of them sons. It didn't feel strange to hug strangers and when she left, she felt a sense of comfort. But out in the darkened parking lot, the dark night cold and humid, Sarah could feel where her tears had dried on her cheeks when the breeze blew toward her. It was her reminder of the processing the evening had given her. And of the pain that had subsided for a while.

Driving back to Lawrence, she turned up the radio and replaced sad thoughts of Jenna with the first love in pop songs. She had thought enough about the group. She wanted to find hope in the darkness.

"Well, how did it go?" Ken would ask her the next day.

"It was good," Sarah said, unable to explain to him why she had felt it worthwhile.

"Will you go back?"

She shrugged her shoulders and watched him eat his sandwich. "There was one thing that bothered me about it. I liked being in a group of people who understood, who get what I've been through. But some of them lost their children ten years ago." She shifted her body in the seat at the outdoor café where they ate lunch. "Ten years after Jenna died, I don't want to be that sad. I don't even want to be that sad now."

Ken nodded and listened. What he did best, Sarah knew. And what she wouldn't let him do for her.

She never went back to the support group. She never went to another support group even when she moved back to Chicago. She knew she'd seen enough that it wasn't what she needed. The problem was she couldn't put her finger on exactly what it was she did need. Or wanted.

~ Sisters: The Karma Twist ~

Comfort, Sarah often thought. What does it really mean? Was it the new couch she had bought for her family room that she could sink into after a long day of teaching and coaching tennis? Or was comfort something one couldn't point out, something that wasn't material?

She looked at Barbara's life with her family. It looked comfortable. A nice house and a sense of warmth when Sarah walked into it. But was it comfortable for them? She tried to scratch that thought as she rubbed the back of Mairzy's ears. What had brought her comfort in the years since Jenna died?

One summer day after Sarah finished graduate school, she sat at her parents' kitchen table, the very one she grew up eating at, with her mother. In front of them Arlene had spread out the family silver on old dish towels and she polished it until it gleamed and sparkled in the sun. Sarah simply watched her mother. In all the years of her life at the house, she had never seen her mother polish the silver. She hardly ever saw the silver. But on this day her mother went at it as if there was a reward at the end for the best polished silver in town. Sarah watched, her eyes going from her mother's face to her hands that moved quickly and urgently across the silver. She tried to see if Arlene was gritting her teeth. Surely this wasn't how people typically polished silver, was it?

Arlene never asked her for help. Sarah never offered. They sat there in silence on a Thursday afternoon in June as if this was a completely routine happening at the McCall house.

Later, Sarah asked Barbara about it. "Did your mom ever polish silver? Or does she now?"

"Oh, girl, did my mom ever!" Barbara laughed. "Haven't you ever heard about Southern women and polishing silver?"

Sarah tried not to look baffled but she had no clue what Barbara was referring to. Her hands rested on the table in front of her, waiting for her laughing friend to answer.

~ Sisters: The Karma Twist ~

"Southern women polish silver as a way of coping with their sexual frustration." Barbara could barely get the words out before she lost herself in her laughter. Sarah wondered about the last time Barbara had laughed that hard.

"Seriously?" Sarah asked, finding it funny, but not that funny.

"Yes, seriously." Barbara sat up at the table and took a sip of her coffee. "My mom was from Alabama, you might remember, and she always polished the silverware. Once a week. One of my cousins told me about it and I then figured out my parents weren't having sex anymore."

Sarah refused to believe that's what it was about. It made more sense that it was about Jenna. If her mother never polished the silver before, unless it was just before a big gathering at the house, why would she do it what seemed like weekly now? If it was about sex, she didn't want to know about it.

We all need comfort, Sarah though, rubbing Mairzy's belly. And wherever we find it, we grab it. If that was where her mother found it, in production, in feeling like she could control something since she couldn't control what Jenna chose to do, then Sarah had to let her do what she needed to do.

Where did she find comfort for herself though? Sarah wasn't sure how to answer that question. She wished she had someone who had walked her grief path with her, someone who could give her a little reminder of how far she had come. She didn't keep journals. No one person had walked the whole way with her. Ken was long gone from her life. And she hadn't been around her parents for much of it. Maybe she wasn't supposed to remember.

She let her head rest on the back of the couch behind her, still keeping Mairzy happy. Jenna would have remembered. It didn't matter now. Life was different. She couldn't change it as much as she wished it would be different.

*****

Does hope show itself all at once? Sarah wondered, walking through the halls during the first passing period. She watched the kids doing all the important things in passing periods that all high school students do. Switching out books, notebooks, and folders. Catching up with crushes. All the things that seemed important at the time. But what about Jenna?

In the beginning, in her first years of teaching, Sarah thought about Jenna a lot when she was at school, wondering what got missed. Over the years she learned to let go of that. She would never truly know what happened but she realized that there were many students for whom she could make a difference. Yet part of her wondered about hope. If a person felt no hope and then one day, somehow, that hope came back, did it come all at once or did it show just glimmers at first, enough to help someone out of bed.

What about her own grief experience? She dug into her mental archives, trying to recall those first years. Graduate school, life, grief. It was one in the same, wasn't it?

*****

Someone suggested she see a therapist. Now she couldn't remember who. Was it one of her professors at KU? Maybe it was her adviser. It was probably Ken. Ultimately, did it really matter who it was? Just like the support group, she knew she should try it at least once.

"Oh hell, I wouldn't do it," Kayla said, a pen in her hand as she readied to grade a series of papers. "That was the worst experience. My mom made me see one before I went to college. She wanted to make sure I was 'well adjusted.' That was her phrase, not mine."

Sarah went anyway. She wasn't looking forward to telling her sister's story. In fact, she wasn't even sure why she was there at all. How could a therapist help her feel better? Heck, she didn't know what the point of therapy was anyway. She never knew anyone in her life who'd been to therapy. And she certainly wasn't going to tell her parents she was going. She could picture the conversation now:

"Are you okay?" her mother would ask, motioning for Frank to get on the phone. "Maybe you should come home."

"No no no," Sarah would try to explain. "I'm fine. Everyone seems to think I need therapy since Jenna died. I don't know why."

"Are you sure you're okay?" her father would ask as they held the phone between then. She could see his worried brow. His eyebrows always made a funny shape when he got worried.

"Are you depressed?" her mother would ask pushing into the conversation in a place where it probably wasn't her turn to speak. Sarah knew she was reading up on depression and suicide. They all were. And that made them all paranoid.

"I'm just sad," she would finally say. At least she knew that would keep them quiet because they were sad, too.

But it wasn't worth the conversation, so instead Sarah went off to a local therapist in Lawrence without telling anyone but Ken and Kayla.

A bearded man sat on the chair across from her, his notepad on his lap, a pen in his hand. Sarah wondered how old he was, trying to sneak peeks at his diplomas on the walls. He didn't look much older than her.

"So what brings you here?" he asked, holding out his hands as if to throw a beach ball into her lap.

Sarah wanted to laugh. At first she wondered why it wasn't written on her head that her sister had killed herself. Really, she didn't know why she was there. She would have preferred working on a big project she had due.

Instead, she took a deep breath and said, "My sister Jenna killed herself eight months ago."

Dr. Thomas sat back in his chair. She wasn't sure if that was good or bad. Maybe she wasn't supposed to tell him Jenna died by suicide. He looked at her for what felt like several minutes before he spoke again. "I'm really sorry."

So help me? she wanted to ask him. I need you to help me. I need you to lead me.

He got up from his chair, putting down his notepad and pen, and walked to the window, leaving Sarah sitting there. She had no idea what was going on. Was this normal? This guy came recommended by someone else. What was his deal?

"Um, aren't you going to help me?" she finally asked, a little shyly.

He stood with his hands on top of his head and shook his head. "I can't."

How could a therapist not help? Sarah wondered. She was baffled beyond belief at this point.

"I just can't." He turned back to her, lowering his arms to his sides. "There's no charge for today. I'm sorry. I can't help you."

~ Sisters: The Karma Twist ~

As Sarah left his office, more confused than when she went in, she had no idea that this would be the first of many experiences where someone couldn't help her because of his or her own issues about suicide. And so she was back alone on the road.

CHAPTER 23

Laundry. Although Sarah's father often said that death and taxes were the two constants in life, Sarah thought laundry was the one constant in her life. No matter what else she had to do on Sunday, there always was the laundry to take care of. It was worse during tennis season when she was gone most of Friday and Saturday. That meant not only did she have to do laundry on Sunday, but she had papers to grade, lessons to plan, a house to clean, and the list went on. Mairzy was a constant, too, always waiting for her to get home, never seemingly sad that he was alone most of the time.

"I can get you a friend," Sarah would tell him as he lay by her feet while she sat on the couch folding an endless stash of t-shirts. "Just because I'm alone doesn't mean you have to be alone."

She'd been out on a date the night before. Not the wisest decision, she realized as she walked out the door the previous evening, looking at everything stacked at her front door waiting for her. Nevertheless, she tried to make the most of it and forget about what was awaiting her at home.

His name was Jerry. He was Barbara's neighbor. "He had a wife," she had whispered over the dinner table two weeks before. "I guess she just up and left him for a woman one day."

Sarah stared at her friend. "Is that good or bad if you are a man and get left for a woman rather than another man?"

Barbara had shrugged her shoulders. "Well, there's not really any direct competition," she reminded Sarah who only nodded in agreement. She worried about everything. This was Barbara's neighbor; what if it went wrong? Did she have anything in common with a man who worked in sales and traveled the world? She begged Barbara to set them up at her house where the atmosphere was controlled.

But Barbara refused. "You need to go out. You teach, you coach, you have no life. Go out and have a good time."

It wasn't a good time. Sarah wished it had been. She wished she hadn't been wishing, while she sat across a table from him, that she was home with Mairzy, eating a bowl of spaghetti left over from the team dinner two nights before. She didn't care how much the steak cost, she wanted to be in her pajamas relaxing after a long day of coaching her girls to a win in the Lakehurst Invitational.

Worse, she had no idea what Barbara had told him about her. That meant half the evening was about making conversation. "So how many brothers and sisters do you have?" he finally asked. Sarah felt her heart slip out of her body, down to the floor, and slither out of the restaurant. She wanted to call to it and tell it what a wimp it was, deserting her when she needed it most. But it was gone and she was left to answer the question.

She wished the waiter would come by. She wished anyone would walk by. She wondered what else she could use for a distraction. She was stuck.

"I have a brother and I had a sister," she finally said, watching him as he finished chewing his piece of steak.

"Had?" he asked, wiping his mouth with his napkin. "I'm not sure what that means."

"She died," Sarah said. She knew there was no getting out of this one. There was no way to phrase it. She didn't want to lie. Heck, maybe he already knew from Barbara anyway.

"Her sister killed herself," Barbara would say nonchalantly as if she was asking her husband to pick up milk and bread at the grocery store. That was how Barbara handled things. With ease and grace. Sarah felt like a tennis ball bouncing against a wall when she tried to handle things. She bumbled them and kept trying to whack them back toward the wall away from her. That's probably why she loved tennis so much. It reminded her of her own life.

"I'm so sorry," Jerry said, adding more butter to his potato. Then he stopped and looked at her. "Do you mind telling me what happened?"

And so it went. Sarah tried to block that night out. It was one of many she tried to smash like an aluminum can. She didn't want to remember them. She wanted them to go away. She didn't want to go down that road. It was too scary for her.

~ Sisters: The Karma Twist ~

*****

Each June Matt and Donna held a birthday party for the twins the Saturday closest to their birthday. And each year Sarah bought the girls a gift, usually something that reminded her of her life with Jenna. They turned eight this year and Sarah managed to find the very doll heads that she and Jenna had destroyed as young girls, first perming their hair and then giving them haircuts. Sarah smiled as she wrapped them, laughing now, but remembering how mad their mother was after she saw what they had done.

"Now you have no reason to play with them," she exclaimed, her hand on her forehead. "I knew I should have waited six years before I had another baby. You two are much too close in age."

The girls didn't get it. They simply stared at her from their spots on Jenna's bedroom floor where they played, the fake hair spread all over the carpet. Arlene McCall made them clean up the dolls, and throw them away, before she vacuumed the rest of the mess. Jenna was in tears, not letting go of her doll.

Now Sarah wondered why she got these dolls. Maybe it was a mistake. The memory in the end hadn't been a happy one although she and Jenna had laughed about it later. She stopped wrapping for a moment, the second box partially surrounded on all sides by the yellow birthday party wrapping paper.

No, she thought, picking the pace back up. This was about happy memories. It wasn't about the sadness. She only wished that Jenna were there to share her excitement in giving the girls the dolls. She knew Matt wouldn't get it. He probably wouldn't even remember. And her parents wouldn't be there. They were long gone to Florida, sending gifts now. Somehow she'd have to muddle along in this without anyone else. Easier said than done.

"Hey Sis," Matt said, wrapping his arm around her after she dropped the gifts in the stack with the others and made her way into the kitchen.

"Hi," Sarah said, knowing the arm hug was as much as she would ever get from her brother.

The conversation was cut short by his friend Bill who walked in the door. And Sarah was left to fend for herself. She felt like a stranger with her brother and his family. This wasn't how she pictured her future. It wasn't how she pictured Jenna's future, the nonexistent one. But she guessed that nothing had changed for Matt. She was sure it was as he wanted it. But this wasn't how she wanted it. She missed her family. She missed her parents. But she knew that for Matt, he would never get it. And her parents hurt too much to bring up what they felt they had lost.

CHAPTER 24

So often she knew people thought their relationship was perfect– hers and Jenna's. And the one time she attended one of those survivor of suicide support groups, she never heard a bad word uttered about the one who died. Even when they were sick, the mental illness that set in and took so many lives, the family members talked of their love and not the difficulties that the mental illness introduced to the family.

She couldn't only remember the good times. That wouldn't be fair to her memories. It wouldn't make Jenna whole. There was the day they took the train and then the El, a two-hour trip from home, up to Wrigley Field for a late April game to sit in the bleachers. The wind blew hard off the lake and it was cold, making both of them a little crabby. Sarah wasn't sure how the argument started. And without Jenna there to remind her, and probably to taunt her that she had started it, she probably never would. But they ended up not speaking to each other for the bulk of the game. It wasn't until the ride home, now feeling much longer than two hours since they weren't speaking, that Sarah almost stepped on Jenna getting on the train and Jenna had elbowed her back. And smiled. Sarah knew then all was forgotten.

It was far from perfect, she thought. Is there any relationship that's perfect? She wondered. Then she would laugh to herself.

Ken. Sarah hated to think about him. He'd tried so hard to be there for her. He didn't quite understand her road though. He wanted to get married after graduate school. He saw a future in the suburbs with a slew of kids. What he didn't get was that for Sarah that dream had flown out the window after Jenna died and she didn't think she could get it back.

"You love me though?" he always asked. "I know you do. So why won't you marry me?"

Sarah would stand there, not able to put into words the emotions she felt. If she didn't understand them herself, how could she explain them to Ken? He read stacks of books on what it was like to lose a loved one to suicide.

Often he would ask Sarah questions randomly: Do you feel guilty? Do you feel depressed? Or, why don't you open the bakery anyway?

"No," she would say, "How can I open a bakery without Jenna? That was our dream, not my dream alone. The point was we were going to do it together." She'd walk away from him, a stack of plates in her hands, ready to set the table for their friends, Rachel and John, who joined them for dinner at least once a week. "I don't want to do it on my own."

Ken would drop the subject and Sarah found she needed that time to gather herself together before Rachel and John arrived. When their friends arrived, she wanted to laugh and be silly. She was tired of trying to figure out why Jenna hanged herself, why she missed out on the future. At some point she knew she would never truly understand and she was slowly reaching that place. Instead, Sarah now tried to figure out how to make her own life happy again. How she could create her own hope even without Jenna.

She loved Ken's blue eyes, and the small things he did for her like the flowers that he brought her on Friday afternoons before they went out to dinner. The smile that made her melt. But she couldn't give him what he wanted. She tried. She wasn't sure he truly knew that she tried nor did she think she could explain it to him. Instead, she had ended the relationship right after graduation when she knew she was moving back to Chicago to teach and he stayed in Kansas for an assistant coach basketball job at a small college.

"You could have gotten a job in Kansas City," he said, watching her pack up her apartment.

She continued to pack and he continued to beg. When he'd leave the apartment each night she would cry. But she knew she couldn't do it, mostly because she didn't think it was fair to him. Or at least that's what she thought. If he truly understood what she was going through, she would think, and he said he did, then he would know that she couldn't get married. She couldn't have kids. She couldn't do any of it without her sister.

But Ken persisted until Sarah found a teaching job in the Chicago area. Slowly he faded away, working in his coaching job in Kansas City, her teaching high school English in the Chicago suburbs. She was grateful that her first year of teaching took up much of her time and left her less time, the third year after Jenna died, to think about what she had lost. She knew somehow she had to get back into life. Somehow she had to go on. But the only way she knew to do it was to work. And work some more.

Her first year of teaching left her emotionally and physically exhausted. No one knew what she had been through and she didn't want them to know. Her students had no idea either, not that it was ever something one discussed with one's students anyway. They didn't think teachers had lives outside of school. She knew that from her own experience as a student when she always was shocked to see them at places like the grocery store. Did they really eat? Have spouses? Homes? Children?

But in that first year she was grateful for something to consume her. Some of it she didn't anticipate though.

It was in the late fall of her second year teaching, right after tennis season ended. Sarah sat at her desk catching up on grading she had put off while she took the girls to compete at the state meet. She thought all the students had left for the afternoon. At least they had left her classroom, although some still hung around each day appearing to have nowhere to go. Sarah was usually long gone to the athletic part of the building by then.

Someone opened her door and she looked up from her computer where she entered the grades of the papers she had just reviewed.

"Hey Ms. McCall," Jarrod Smith said.

"Hey Jarrod," Sarah said, smiling at him. He dropped his backpack on the desk closest to her and slipped into the desk itself. She was used to Jarrod coming around. He was one of the ones who liked to spend his lunchtime in her classroom, often just talking about life. Sometimes he would mention girls he was too afraid to ask out, Sarah encouraging him to do it anyway, and other times he would want to discuss whatever they were reading or writing about in class. There were a few others but Jarrod was the one she saw the most of. "What brings you by this afternoon?"

"I need some help," he said.

Sarah took her hands off the computer keyboard and pulled her chair toward her desk in front of her. "What's up?" She fully expected he would want to continue their discussion of Hemingway's *The Old Man and the Sea* from earlier that day.

Jarrod looked around. He was clearly uncomfortable. Sarah tried not to let him see she was getting uncomfortable. She didn't know where this was going. She peeked to her right and saw the door into the office pod was open. She felt a little safer. She didn't expect Jarrod to do anything so much as she thought he might say something. She just wasn't sure what.

"I don't know how to say this."

Sarah dropped her hands to her lap.

"I want to die."

She felt her heart drop all the way to her stomach. She had begun to think he had a crush on her, something that wouldn't have surprised her, but to hear he was suicidal, that surprised and scared her. Jarrod had no idea about her sister. No one at the school knew.

Suddenly she found herself flipping through her mental filing cabinet. She didn't know much about suicide beyond what she had read in that first year after Jenna died. They didn't teach them anything in school about suicidal students except to refer them to the counseling staff. There wasn't time now to think anymore. Jarrod waited for a response.

Sarah got up and walked to the desk next to him where she sat down. She thought of Jenna. She wished she knew what to say. She wished she had some clue about what to do. "So what's going on?" she asked.

Jarrod sat forward and began to discuss the pressure he felt from his parents to do well in school. What Sarah heard wasn't any different than any other student. But losing Jenna had taught her that there had been something missing. There had been something they all didn't get. Maybe by listening to Jarrod she would get it.

While she heard the clock tick on the wall to her left, she didn't dare look at it. She knew she had to give Jarrod her full attention. She tried to keep her hands in her lap but they shook. She was afraid. For Jarrod. And for herself. She let him talk. She listened. Finally, she knew there was nothing more she could do for him.

"Look Jarrod, I'm happy to help you but I think you need something more than I can give you," Sarah said, trying to talk calmly. It was almost like those first days of teaching when she was unsure she was saying the right words or making sense. She felt her entire body shake the first two weeks. She knew the students picked up on it despite her brave front.

This was no different. It was new territory in many ways. It wasn't new because she lost Jenna. It was new because she wanted to make sure Jarrod didn't travel that same road as her sister. And she didn't want him to know what she'd been through. It was irrelevant.

"Okay," Jarrod said. "Counseling office?"

Sarah couldn't help but smile. "You okay with that?"

He nodded. "I just thought I'd rather talk to you than them."

Sarah smiled again. "I know. You see me everyday. It is usually easier to talk to someone you have daily contact with."

After leaving him with the counselor she felt the most confident in, she walked back to her classroom, taking deep breaths. It wasn't enough though. She flopped into her desk chair, the wheels sending her slightly backward, and the emotions erupted in a way she didn't expect. She'd tried hard to hold it in but once she could let go, she couldn't stop it.

Jenna, she cried silently.

But she couldn't even think anything else. Just Jenna's name.

"Oh, what happened?" Sarah heard a voice and looked up to see another teacher, Reba Peterson, poking her head in the door. "Are you okay?"

Sarah got up, looking for the box of tissues that is standard in classrooms everywhere. "Yeah, I think so."

Reba stood in the doorway. "Do you want to talk about it?"

Sarah tried to wave it off. Where would she start? Where would she end?

But the counselor saved the day, showing up at the door just a few minutes later. "We released Jarrod to his parents," she said. "They're on their way with him for an evaluation."

Sarah nodded acknowledgment.

"Oh, did you have a suicidal student?" Reba asked. "That's a tough one."

"She did a good job," the counselor said. "He said he felt a lot better after talking to you."

~ Sisters: The Karma Twist ~

All Sarah could do was nod her head. She leaned on the table that held the box of tissues and held her arms crossed in front of her. It was too cold for short sleeves. She knew that when she chose that dress this morning but she had done it anyway. And now she was cold, tired, and stressed out.

"Are you okay?" the counselor asked, glancing at her watch.

"I'm fine," Sarah finally said. "I'm just glad he's okay."

Before she left the school, Sarah picked up the phone in the back office and called Barbara. "Do you think I could join your family for dinner?"

And when she arrived, she grabbed the kids and hugged them so long that they tried to wiggle away from her. "I think you just scared them," Barbara said. "Are you okay?"

There would be several other suicidal students over her seven years of teaching. A few cutters. Several where she was given a note asking for their homework and told they were in the hospital. Sometimes when they came back, they told her they had attempted suicide. She tried to listen as she did for Jarrod. The day he graduated he hugged her as he left the ceremony with his family.

"Thanks, Ms. McCall," was all he said. Sarah only smiled. She knew what he meant. And then she looked toward the sky and thought of Jenna. She had changed. She never saw herself as a bad person or an uncaring person but losing Jenna had definitely made her more aware of the vast pain in the world.

CHAPTER 25

Sarah knew there was a joke at the school about her and the physical education teacher Allison Johnson. "No one can decide who's hotter," at least one of her boy students would say each semester. "You or Ms. Johnson."

The first time she heard this, she held a pen in her hand and she almost ended up writing on her face. She had felt her skin turn hot. She was red for sure. She put her hand on her face forgetting her pen was there.

But the student usually continued, "It's her in those short shorts or you in your tennis skirt."

This was a running joke with all her friends but it took her awhile to get there. And only was she able to get there by laughing about herself. She didn't know Allison Johnson very well. Allison didn't coach any sports and left as soon as the day was out, the same part of the day when Sarah arrived in the athletic department to put on her tennis skirt.

"Well, who won?" Jeff, Barbara's husband, would ask each semester when Sarah mentioned it.

"Jeffrey!" Barbara would contest. Then they all would laugh. "But I'd rather have my friend be the hottest teacher in school than the one they made fun of."

"It's easier to talk about with a glass of wine in hand," Sarah would remind them, reaching for her goblet.

It was another day that Mark hadn't stopped by her classroom that Sarah ran into Allison Johnson. Although she had talked to him the evening before, she was surprised he didn't at least come say hi. The school year was coming to a close and they were all busy finishing the semester. But this was out of his routine.

Every spring the school was hot. It never failed. When they came back in the fall, they froze, in the spring they sweltered. Sarah always believed it gave everyone an opportunity to wear their new warm clothes in the fall and break out the shorts in the spring. This day was no exception as she walked through the hall to Mark's classroom. Even in her pencil skirt she sweated and thought about how much she would hate to be a man on a day like this.

As she turned the corner to enter Mark's room, she saw a pair of legs on a desk in the front row. She peeked around and saw they belonged to Allison Johnson who laughed one of those throaty laughs one always hears from a woman who is seeking a man. Just like the movies, Sarah thought, backing away.

But it was too late. As she walked quickly away, Mark walked out of the room. Somehow he managed to see her. "Hey Sarah," he called. Sarah stopped and turned, taking a deep breath and placing her hands on her hips. She wished he hadn't seen her. How could she get out of this? "Hey," he said. "Why didn't you come in?"

"I hadn't seen you yet today," she said, trying to be calm. Cool. Collected. But the sweat beaded and dripped down her back. It wasn't working. And she stumbled over her words.

"I know. I had to grade papers but I thought maybe we could get together later."

"Okay," she said, still wanting to get away. "Just let me know. I better get back to my seventh period's essays."

She turned to walk and he called her name again. She stopped but didn't turn around this time. "The baseball banquet is next week. I need to talk to you about it."

"We'll do it later," she said, waving him off. "I need to go."

She finished grading when she reached her classroom and her desk. She flopped herself into her chair, slipping off her shoes. She knew she wanted to cry. She knew she couldn't do this. She knew she was a mess. Why did she allow herself to go down this road with him? It had been a mistake. She tried but she couldn't do it. And now she had to get out of the school before anyone saw her completely lose it.

She held her breath almost the entire walk from her classroom to the faculty parking lot. No one stopped her. No one saw her. Once in her car, she found her cell phone and called Barbara. "I need help," she cried.

"Go home and get Mairzy and then come over," Barbara said. No questions asked. She knew Barbara would figure it out. She probably waited for it.

And when they arrived an hour later, Barbara handed her a glass of water. "No wine for you. If I know you, you've been crying the whole way here and now you're dehydrated." Sarah took the glass and curled up in a corner of the living room couch. The house was quiet and Sarah wondered if she was in the right place.

"Where are the kids?" she asked, looking around.

Barbara slid into the other corner of the couch. "Girl, you never come over this early. Today is their daycare afternoon for my mental health." She paused and tapped Sarah's bare foot. "What happened? What did he do? Or better yet, what do you think he did?"

"I can't do it. I can't do it." The well opened up. "I tried but I can't do this road."

Barbara got the tissues and didn't say anything. She didn't cross her arms as if she knew better. She let Sarah spew it all out. And then she waited in the pauses, as if she read the spaces between the words, for more. Sarah thought she was long past done when Barbara finally spoke.

"It's abandonment. You know that. It's nothing new. It's what you've been doing all along."

Sarah began to cry again. "I can't. I can't. He's going to leave me like Jenna did." She blew her nose.

"And you're going to make that decision for him before he even gets the chance to?"

Sarah didn't want to hear it. She tucked herself inside herself. It was easier that way. But Barbara knew her too well.

"Listen," she said, looking out the window at the sunshine on the warm day, "I know it was painful the way Jenna left you. I know it hurts because it completely altered your life plans. But it's not going to happen again. Yes, people come in and out of your life, but you know that this wasn't a typical event."

"How do you know that it won't happen again?" Sarah snapped, Mairzy settling in at her feet. She reached down to rub the top of his head. "It's become part of my life. Part of my reality. Part of my vocabulary,"

"And for ten years, you've let it run your life," Barbara reminded her. "You've let this fear of abandonment grip you so tight that you can't let it go."

"I'm not one of those women at that support group in Kansas City," Sarah cried. "I don't feel guilty. I'm not going to let it run my life."

"But it still is running your life," Barbara said, a gentle smile on her face. "It's why you don't have a family. It's why you didn't open the bakery anyway. It's why you aren't in a relationship." She paused and laughed. "The hottest teacher in school doesn't have a romantic relationship. Thank God they don't think you're a lesbian."

Sarah couldn't help but laugh although then it made her hiccup. Barbara got up to refill Sarah's water glass but still spoke to her from the kitchen. "You're not letting go of Jenna by not letting go of the fear of abandonment. Jenna is still with you. She always will be. And you have the memories." Barbara walked back into the living room with the glass filled with ice and water this time. "You know that. But I think that if Jenna were here, Jenna as I knew her, would tell you to get on with it. She would say to you that she wants you to be happy. She never meant to hurt you with her death."

"Why aren't you a therapist?" Sarah asked her friend after the hiccups subsided.

Barbara smiled. "This is more fun. I'd tell too many people to get over it and probably would be sued. I don't know why we can't tell people what they really need to know." She shook her head. "Here's what you have to do. You have to make abandonment your friend."

"Did you see that on Oprah?"

"No, I actually just made it up," Barbara laughed. "I really did. But think about it. It's your enemy. You run from it each time it happens. You won't even let it near you. Why do you do that? It's almost like a denial that as long as you don't let it near, you keep running. Don't keep running. Don't let it get to you."

"But how?"

~ Sisters: The Karma Twist ~

"I didn't say I had all the answers," Barbara laughed. "That's why you're not paying me. All I know is that somewhere in that noggin of yours, you have the ability to push yourself and figure this out. It can't be any more difficult than running those suicides on that hot tennis court or running six miles on a track. It's all mind over matter."

Sarah knew she was right. Barbara almost always was right. But she didn't know how she could do it. As the kids began to arrive home, she knew she had to leave. "You can stay for dinner," Barbara said, giving her a hug.

"No," Sarah said. "I have papers to grade."

"But you'll be free to go swimming with us soon," her friend giggled. "I got our pool pass today. Another summer at the 'hood pool with the kids."

The thought of summer, of the warmth, of sitting by Barbara's neighborhood pool filled with kids and moms on a weekday afternoon gave her a temporary reprieve. She got in her car at least feeling okay for the moment. The closer she got to home though, the sadness returned.

When her cell phone buzzed, she thought it might be Mark and actually felt disappointed to look down and see it was Barbara. "I know you don't want it to be me," Barbara said, "but I just wanted to remind you that you don't know why Allison was in his classroom. Stop creating storylines that aren't true if you don't know what they are!"

Sarah knew she wasn't going to grade papers. Her focus was shot for the day. She fed Mairzy and made her way to her bedroom, then remembered that she needed to get the clean laundry out of the dryer she'd forgotten the day before. But before she could reach the laundry room between the garage and kitchen, her cell phone rang again. It was Mark.

"Hey," he said, "you ran off before I could talk to you more."

"I had papers to grade," she reminded him.

"I've got my own," he said. "If I bring over a pizza tonight to your house, do you want to have a grading party?"

She knew he was serious. And she knew she couldn't do it. "I'm too exhausted," she said. That was true. "Can we do it another night?"

"I'm sure my grading won't go away before tomorrow," he chuckled. She sensed he thought he made funny jokes. Or maybe on any other day she might have laughed at them. He paused before speaking again. "Are you sure you're okay?"

Sarah took a deep breath, holding the phone away from face, and straightened her back. "Yeah, I'm just tired. End of the year exhaustion." She didn't want him to know. She couldn't go there tonight.

"Okay, well, I'll stop and see you tomorrow so you don't think I'm not there. If Allison Johnson hadn't stopped by today to give me the stuff for the baseball banquet, I would have had time to see you."

Sarah didn't react. She knew she couldn't. He could never know what she was struggling with. It was enough that Barbara knew. No one else needed to know her challenges. With the call ended, she pulled her clothes out of the dryer and placed them on top in a pile. As she moved them, she felt relief that Allison had been there to drop off the letters for the athletes. Sarah had forgotten that was something she did do for the athletic department although she always left Sarah's in a box.

That relief turned to sadness and her energy slipped from her, leaving her standing lifeless in her laundry room. Sarah placed her head on the clean clothes, relishing the clean scent of laundry. But she couldn't move for what felt like several minutes. And when she finally did make it to the bedroom, she dropped the clothes on a chair, slipped out of her clothes, and fell into her bed, Mairzy lying on the floor next to her. No one had to know she cried herself to sleep that night.

The morning was worse. It started out okay. She felt fine when she woke up. She thought maybe she could conquer the world again. But it disappeared as soon as she finished her shower. She turned a photo of Jenna on her dresser around. "I can't think about you," she said out loud, a tinge of anger in her voice. "I know I have to forgive you for leaving but I'm too angry about how my life has turned out right now."

Sarah knew no one at school would have any clue what she was coping with in her life. Outside of the lack of a boyfriend, everyone thought she had it together. She was a good teacher. She had built a strong tennis program. They didn't know what her life outside of school consisted of and she didn't believe anyone needed to know.

The papers waited where she left them the night before when she entered the darkened classroom. It was a coffee day for sure. She had to shut the emotions down. Trying to figure out how to make friends with abandonment was proving more difficult than she thought. But it was no different than the self talk she lectured her tennis girls about each season.

"Look, half of this is in your heads," she would tell them after practice at least once a week as they all sat together on the court drinking water and resting after the workout had ended. "It's mind over matter. You have to believe you can do it. You have to believe that you are winners."

It was no different with abandonment. Sarah pictured herself pulling up a chair and letting the word abandonment climb into it next to her. "Friends," she was saying. "We're going to be friends." Abandonment didn't talk back. It didn't smile or acknowledge her at all. It simply sat there. It wasn't simple to let it sit there. No, maybe it wasn't for *it*. It wasn't for her to let it bother her though.

She kept glancing over toward it. "Mind over matter," she mumbled to herself, waiting for the first students to file in. "I need to believe my own advice." It worked for her tennis girls. That's what got them to state. If she could use it in her own life, then she had another lesson she could share with them.

Instead of the students though, Mark did his usual head poking. "Hey," he said, "thought I'd check on you. Are you talking to yourself?"

"I do all the time," she said, starting to say that abandonment was sitting next to her but stopped herself before she did. Surely he would have no idea what she talked about. "I just try not to let anyone see me do it."

He sat on his usual desk. "Listen, I really want to see you tonight. And I'm serious, even if we grade papers the entire time, I'm happy to be there with you. Will you let me bring you a pizza?"

Sarah wanted to say no. She wanted to tell him that she was busy. She wanted to say that she couldn't have anyone over to grade papers because she needed complete silence. But it would all be a lie.

"Don't let Jenna's death continue to rule your life," she heard Barbara saying in her head. "I don't care what you say, it's what you're doing. She wouldn't want you to be unhappy. She loved you more than anyone else. The last thing she wanted to do was hurt you. But she was too afraid of what was happening to her that she couldn't reach out. And she couldn't feel beyond her own pain."

Barbara was right. She always was right. Well, most of the time. But she was this time. "Don't push him away," she added as Mark sat there and waited.

"Okay," Sarah said, "as long as we really do grade papers."

"We'll have plenty of time for fun once school lets out in a few weeks," he said. "And it's going to be a fun summer."

Sarah would have let her head fall to her desk if her students hadn't started to come in by then. No, she thought, abandonment is my friend. She turned to her side and thought about abandonment sitting there quietly. Maybe if she let abandonment sit there long enough, it would go away. Maybe she wouldn't need it at all. Then she began to wonder if it was female or male. And that's when she knew she had to get to work.

*****

Sarah wrung her hands that evening waiting for Mark to arrive. She tried to grade as many papers as she could before he rang the doorbell but she couldn't focus. She was tired from the day before. She was tired from the current day. She really wanted to take a nap. Going to bed early again seemed like a great idea. She wanted to not think for eight hours. That felt like a luxury after all the emotional upheaval.

"I hope pepperoni is okay," Mark said, balancing a pizza on his right hand and his leather messenger bag over his left shoulder.

"Yep," Sarah said, taking the pizza and letting him follow her in.

She watched him make himself at home in the living room next to where she worked. "Should we eat first?" she asked, watching him pull out his papers and his laptop.

"Isn't that always how it should go?" he asked her. "Eat first, do everything else later?"

Sarah laughed, plates in her hand. "I'm not going to respond to that one. But if you want pizza, here's a plate."

They sat together at the breakfast bar, both of them continually turning their stools as if they couldn't sit still. "You know what I hate most about grading?" Sarah asked, grabbing another slice of pizza, "It's that I have to sit still to do it. I hate to sit still."

~ Sisters: The Karma Twist ~

Mark laughed, holding his finger out to let her know he was going to add to that when he was done chewing. "I'd rather have my teeth pulled most days than grade papers."

"Necessary evil of being a teacher," Sarah sighed.

"That's why we have summers off. To recover from the grading."

They were quiet for a while, thinking while they ate. "It feels comfortable to be with you. Do you know that?" he asked, touching the top of her hand next to him.

Sarah smiled. "I know." She had forgotten her fears for the moment. Maybe that was the key. If she stayed in the moment, there was no reason to let abandonment get to her. She wondered where abandonment was anyway. She kept looking for it as if she needed to keep a close eye on it until their trust had been built. Abandonment was on the chair across from the couch though. Not too far away. She hoped that Mairzy didn't bark at it. "Friends," she would have to say, "We're friends." Even in the moment, even when she felt calm, abandonment was there. Didn't it have work to do? she wondered. Surely, she wasn't the only one who dealt with it. She looked over at the chair. Maybe this was her personal version and everyone else's looked a little different.

"Why do you keep looking over at the couch?" Mark asked. "It's almost as if you're looking for someone."

Sarah shook her head. "No reason. Habit to look for Mairzy," she lied. Was it really a lie? He didn't need to know about all her fears. Not now. Not ever. This wasn't his battle anyway.

"You've let me come over and grade papers and eat pizza with you," Mark said as he gathered up his things to leave, the clock approaching 10:00 pm, "now will you let me take you out and do something that isn't related to cookies or grading papers?"

Sarah held a stack of essays in her hand. She wasn't expecting that. She was content as things were. Why wasn't he? She didn't know what to say.

"Don't say no," he said. "Don't say no like you have to every other man who has asked you out. Is this some sort of workplace issue? Do I need to find a new school to work at and then you'll go out with me?"

She began to laugh. It sounded preposterous, but then she realized he was serious and a tear slid down her cheek.

"I knew it," he said, wiping it away. "There's something more there. He let his bag slide to the floor. "I'm not leaving until you tell me what it is, even if I don't go home until morning."

"Why?" she asked.

"Because I like you. A lot. And I'm not letting you get away. A woman like you doesn't come around very often. Believe me, I'm nearing forty and I've been around a lot of them. You're very special."

She started to speak but nothing came out. She cleared her throat and pointed. "Over there, on the chair?" Mark looked and saw nothing, then looked back at her.

"What? There's nothing on the chair."

"Abandonment is on the chair over there." She knew he didn't get it. "The word, the emotion. I'm trying to make it my friend." He still wasn't getting it. "It's my biggest challenge since my sister died. It's the reason I'm not married. It's the reason I hardly date." She stopped speaking and began to cry. Embarrassed, she went to find the tissues and brought a handful back with her from the bathroom. "I'm sorry, it's all come to a head over the past few days."

Mark took her hand and held it. "I'm not going anywhere. You know that." She blew her nose with a tissue in her other hand and nodded.

"My friend Barbara said I need to make friends with abandonment and that's why I pointed to it. It's sitting in that chair over there and I'm trying to be okay with it. The more I'm friends with it, the more it won't bother me."

"I don't understand what exactly you're afraid of."

"That if I move forward with my emotions, what I feel for you, that you will leave me one day, not by suicide, but you'll leave me one day like my sister did."

"And you can't get past that?" he asked.

"I can to a point. I did at one time. But then I couldn't let the relationship go further. So I shut down. And the relationship didn't last. I haven't tried since then."

Mark moved closer to her. "I'm not going anywhere. I don't know how to get you to see that though."

"I can't. And that's why you have to let me figure this out on my own."

"I can't help you?" He looked a little perplexed. "I want to help."

"I don't know how to let you help," she said. "I'm not even sure how to help myself."

"But I can be there for you. I mean if this is all it is, I can be there for you."

"You don't get it. It's not such a small thing to me though. It's a big deal."

"I know and I want to help."

Sarah didn't know what to say. She saw Mark's eyes pleading with her, to be with her on this road she had to travel. But did he really understand? Could he really help? What would Barbara say? What would Jenna say?

"I don't know" was all that came out. "I'm sorry. I just don't know."

Mark took a deep breath. He let her hand go. He looked straight ahead and then looked back at her. "I'm here if you need me." He gave her a quick kiss on her forehead before he left, leaving Sarah staring at her closed front door. Alone.

CHAPTER 26

Josh Brown. Sarah could remember him just like it was yesterday. He had spikey blonde hair. He was on the swim team with Jenna although the girls swam in the fall and the boys in the winter. Yet he was always right at Jenna's side when Sarah showed up with the car after tennis practice to pick up her sister.

"He keeps saying he wants to marry me." Jenna would laugh as she dumped her books, her wet towel, and backpack into the backseat, sliding into the front seat next to Sarah.

This was ongoing over a period of time. It felt as if each time Jenna got into the car that swim season, Josh had told her that he was going to marry her one day. And Jenna acted like it would never happen.

"How could he know?" Jenna would ask, waving it off and turning up the radio so she didn't have to talk to Sarah.

Sarah usually let it be but one day she'd had enough and turned the radio down even though one of her favorite bands, Duran Duran, played. "How do you know he doesn't know that he truly wants to marry you one day? How do you know that you won't marry him one day? Are you a fortune teller? Do we have some gypsy in us I don't know about?"

Jenna laughed, reaching for the radio knob but Sarah slapped her hand. She saw Jenna pull it back and look straight ahead. "None of us know what the future holds," Jenna said simply.

After Jenna died, Sarah had wished she had pushed her sister harder to find out what she meant. Was she already fearing for the future?

She now stood in the middle of the food court in the mall with Josh Brown standing next to her. His hair wasn't so spikey now. Sarah thought he was still cute. There was that boyishness to him. And he must have been fearless to continually tell Jenna he would marry her one day.

"You know," Josh said, shaking his head, his hands deep in the pockets of his fleece pullover, "I really thought I would marry Jenna one day."

Sarah smiled. She had been afraid to ask yet she got her answer. And all along her intuition had been right. As the world milled around them, screaming children, shopping bags and all, Sarah hoped that Jenna saw that scene. That she saw that Josh was right. He really had wanted to be with her.

He had two children he said, a boy and a girl. Sarah was glad for him. But she wondered why she couldn't have kids. Why was everyone able to move on but her? No one knew the extent of what Jenna meant to her life though. They had to go on but they hadn't lost a sister. They hadn't lost a piece of themselves like she had.

Why had she taken on Jenna's fear of the future? And how would she free herself of it? As she and Josh parted ways, she tried to picture Jenna walking with her, as two women in their late twenties/early thirties at the mall on a Saturday afternoon. Probably not unlike something they might have done. What would Jenna say to her?

"Don't be stupid. Just because I was afraid, doesn't mean you have to be."

Sarah knew she was right.

*****

Sarah finally trekked to Florida to see her parents in the fifth year after Jenna died. They had been there two years already and were snug as two bugs in their condo that overlooked the Gulf of Mexico.

"We're so happy here," her mom said giddily as she opened the sliding glass door onto their balcony. Sarah felt closed in, having travel eight floors up in the elevator to their place. Everyone placed welcome mats in front of their doors as if that might give the hallway personality.

Sarah stood on the balcony, looking at the sand and water below. It was spring break for her, the only time she could get away besides summer, and the weather was good. The salt air kissed her face. That she could get used to. As she turned to walk back inside though, the box they lived in, like a shoebox shoved onto a shelf with a group of other shoeboxes, she realized she couldn't get comfortable with that.

Her dad waited, his left arm ready for her to walk into. "We've missed you, you know," he said, hugging her shoulder tight.

"I missed you, too," Sarah said, really wanting to say, "Why don't you reach out to me?" She almost felt as if they had let go of their life in Illinois to not ever be remembered again.

That night, out to dinner at their favorite local seafood restaurant, she tried to bring up Jenna. "Why don't you two ever talk about Jenna? I don't even see a photo of her in the condo." Sarah had looked high and low; most of the furniture and photos looked familiar. But nothing, absolutely nothing, of Jenna.

Her mother's face fell. Her father watched her mother's reaction. No one spoke.

"Mom, you're the one who didn't want to erase the memories of her from the house yet now that you've moved, you act like she never existed."

"We miss her more than you will ever know," her mother seethed. "Don't you ever accuse me of acting like she never existed." Arlene McCall looked around as if there might be an escape route somewhere. Sarah could tell her father placed his hand on her thigh, hoping to calm her down. She could see he knew he was going to have to play peacemaker between them. Sarah was glad she had gone with her intuition and not booked a ticket for a full week. It was clear she wouldn't be back any time soon.

That set the tone for her trip. It was more about what wasn't said than what was. Life had changed and it was apparent it was beyond repair in many ways. Sarah always believed anything could be repaired, but since Jenna died, she had come to realize that wasn't always the case. As she lay trying to sleep in the guest room each night, the window open so she could smell the gulf and hear the waves crashing on the shore, she understood the solace they found in their new home.

The last morning she was there, she sat on the balcony with the book she was reading. Her dad walked outside and sat down next to her. "Beautiful day," he said. "Most of them are like this though." Sarah put her book in her lap and waited to hear what else he might say. "Sarah, you know it's been a hard road for all of us. I miss your sister everyday. I miss the future she never had. I miss watching you two and your relationship."

She waited for him to say something else. But he didn't. She thought he opened his mouth to speak again after a long pause but the phone rang

164

and her mother called that it was his friend Glenn calling to see if they were still on for golf the next morning.

Sitting there by herself, Sarah realized it would never be the same with her parents. She knew she wouldn't go back to Florida any time soon. She knew that Jenna never meant to hurt them all with her death but it had changed them in ways no one would have predicted. Or expected.

*****

Kayla had told her back at Kansas that she had watched many families cope with suicide over the years. Her mother had dragged her to what she called a "boat load" of therapists and then there were the support groups. "You wouldn't believe the stuff I've seen," she would almost cackle. "You made the right decision by not going back. Some people never let go."

Even ten years later, Sarah thought about those women in the support group in Kansas City. She thought of them being ten, fifteen, twenty years after the deaths of their children or their spouses. She thought of their sadness. That was the worst. How could they still be sad after so many years? Sarah was twenty-one when Jenna died. She didn't want to spend the rest of her life sad like that. She knew deep inside of her that she could have a happy life. She just wasn't sure how to get there.

The thoughts of these women came at various times. Sometimes she was sad herself and contemplating if she too was doomed for a life of sadness. Other times she was doing well, and just wondered how a person could be that sad for that long period of time.

Barbara was the one constant in Sarah's life and she was the only person Sarah felt, as the years went by, she could still share about Jenna.

"You know," Barbara had said, looking thoughtful as her eyes wandered around her dining room where they once again sat, "I have to wonder about something. You come to me and you say to me something like, 'It's the anniversary of Jenna's death and I feel all these emotions.' But when you think about it, it's not about Jenna anymore. Or at least it shouldn't be about Jenna."

Sarah looked at her. She felt a little stunned. Or was it stung? Was Barbara right? She couldn't answer. They stared at each other over the dining room table, still filled with dishes, including several plates of half-eaten pizza. The table acted as a barrier between them. Sarah couldn't decide if it was a good or bad one.

"You know I meant that in a helpful way, right?" Barbara finally asked, breaking the icy silence.

And Sarah started to cry. "I want to laugh but for some reason I'm crying." She pointed a finger at her face. "I have no idea where this is coming from."

"The pain inside you that you've carried around too long. I know that you never felt guilty about why Jenna killed herself. That's never been an issue with you like I hear it is with many other people." And with that, Sarah thought of those women in the group who couldn't let go of their guilt ranging from not picking up their son as an infant when he was crying to not listening to their husbands when they complained. "But what I hear from you is that you are afraid of the future without Jenna."

Sarah nodded. Barbara was right. She couldn't carry that fear any longer. She felt Jenna telling her to let go and now her best friend told her the same thing. Jenna was gone and Sarah's life had gone on. But now she also should enjoy it.

CHAPTER 27

"You need to include your sister's story in these presentations," Mark said, the morning after she had given a talk for the graduating athletes.

"Why?" Sarah asked him, shaking her head. "I don't know what the connection between my sister and motivation is."

"Your sister killed herself, right?" he asked. Sarah nodded, watching him closely. She didn't mind any feedback, she just wasn't sure if this was relevant feedback.

"You know that. So?"

"She was a high school student. She was an athlete. You two motivated each other. She killed herself and you've gone on to have a lot of success coaching girls tennis. It sounds to me like you need to give your sister a voice."

Sarah leaned back in her chair. "I don't know," she said quietly. "That's been a very personal journey. I'm not sure it's something I could share with everyone." Sarah covered her face with her hands. She didn't want Mark to see she was going to cry. The idea of sharing her sister's story scared her. It had been a long, difficult journey. Treacherous was the word that always came to her when she thought about it. And she thought she'd finally reached a place where she was comfortable with her sister's story. But here Mark had the gall to suggest she share it with everyone?

"I'm sorry, I didn't mean to upset you," he said. Sarah took a deep breath, knowing her students were around the corner waiting to walk into the classroom. She didn't want them to see her cry either. Her right hand shaped into a fist; she held it in front of her mouth and nodded, all she could do to keep the tears from falling.

*****

The Northwestern University campus ran along Lake Michigan. Sarah loved to stand next to the lake, whether it was downtown on a beach or at a park that lined the lake like where she stood, the papers in her hands to register for classes. No one knew that she had applied for the doctoral program in sports psychology. Not even Barbara.

She talked to Jenna, especially as she was filling out the forms, knowing her sister couldn't help her, but bringing Sarah the comfort she needed that someone was listening. Her acceptance came on a hot May day. That afternoon she'd been on the courts with some of the girls on her team.

"Please," they begged, "we want to be outside. Will you come play with us?" Spring fever always hit hardest in May with a few weeks left of the semester. Sarah reluctantly agreed, knowing that the stack of papers on her desk waiting to be graded wouldn't go away until she went through all of them. Still, she couldn't say no. The girls were the reason she was who she was, almost as much as her relationship with Jenna.

But as she stood on the hot court, waiting for Hayley to lob the ball over the net back at her, a butterfly swooped down on Sarah and almost nailed her in the cheek.

"Coach!" Sally called. "What was that?"

Sarah, mesmerized, although her face stung from where the butterfly tapped her, couldn't believe it came back and flew around her face. She couldn't move. After a moment, she knew it was Jenna. While she'd always heard stories about how loved ones came back in other forms, this was the first time she had felt Jenna's presence in this way. Or was it the first time she was aware of it?

"Hey, Sis," Sarah said, "nice to see you."

And with another swoop, the butterfly was gone, leaving Hayley waiting with the green ball in one hand and her racket in the other. "Ready, Coach?"

"Give me a minute," Sarah called back to her, taking a deep breath and smiling as she watched the sky. The butterfly was long gone but the idea that Jenna had been there left her feeling...satisfied.

"Coach? Did you call that butterfly 'Sis'?" Sally asked, walking over from the other court.

For the first time, Sarah didn't hesitate. She smiled instead. "It was my sister." She proceeded to tell Sally that she knew her sister who had died had just visited her.

"Wow," Sally said, smiling. "That's really cool."

When Sarah got home that afternoon, in the mailbox among the junk mail, was her acceptance letter into the doctoral program at Northwestern. As she read the letter, she smiled although tears flowed freely down her face. Jenna let her know she supported her. Sarah wished they were in the room together. She knew, even at thirty-one years old, she and her sister would be jumping around and dancing, celebrating Sarah's new journey. Sarah wasn't quite sure where the journey would take her. But she knew she was ready for it.

Instead, she drove over to Barbara's with a bottle of wine and pizza for the family to celebrate. "Dinner's on me," she announced, barging into the house, Barbara looked frazzled on the couch where one of the kids had been arguing with her. "I got into the sports psychology doctoral program at Northwestern."

"You what?" Barbara asked, looking dazed before everything clicked together. "YOU WHAT?!" And she and Sarah danced around the living room with the kids.

As Sarah sat that night with her friend and her family, she knew this was what life was about. The super happy moments sometimes were few and far between, but Sarah was bound not to miss them anymore than she had over the past ten years. She knew that going forward all would be different.

CHAPTER 28

There were two parts of Sarah moving forward in her grief after ten years. She could feel a shift. She began to understand that even though her life had changed, it was still hers. But going to the baseball banquet still left her paralyzed with fear. In those last weeks of school, Mark popped his head in only to say, "Just checking to make sure you're still here" and then he would leave when Sarah smiled at him. She only smiled because she didn't know what to say. She had allowed him to see a part of her that no one knew about.

Except her friends. It wasn't that she was afraid of what he might do with it, that didn't worry her at all. She had allowed herself to be vulnerable to some extent. She gave up her control. That's what scared her. Abandonment still followed her around. Or at least they were walking side by side. Sometimes when she was alone, she had conversations with abandonment. Wasn't that part of what friendship was about? No, it couldn't be friendship, she'd realize, friendship was reciprocal and she and abandonment certainly didn't have that. What could she offer abandonment? The point of making friends with it was so that it would go away. But maybe that's what she could give abandonment, peace so that it could move on.

She wasn't thrilled to go to the baseball banquet but she did it because she had promised Mark she would be there. She knew it wasn't just important to her but also the booster club because her cookies had been so popular.

She kept Jenna's death in perspective. Jenna led her to these things. She knew that. They probably would have happened much sooner if she had been open to them. But maybe not. Sarah now understood that life was about the current moment. A synchronicity of how things came together. She could reflect back and look forward but she couldn't get stuck in either place for long. She rooted herself in the present although she was grateful for the memories of the past and the possibilities of the future.

As she walked into the restaurant where the baseball banquet was held, Mark stood there at the door greeting everyone. Sarah braced herself. She didn't know why. He wanted to support her. If she had told him what to do, he would have done it. But she didn't have any answers last week nor did she have any now. And she didn't want to answer any questions.

When she walked in, although he was talking to someone else, he touched her arm as if he didn't want to her to go anywhere. She stood and waited while he chatted with some parents. And when they left to go inside, he turned his attention to her.

"I'm glad you came," he said, looking older in a tie.

"Thank you," Sarah said.

"Everyone is glad the cookie lady will be here."

Sarah laughed. "They probably think I'm some little old lady, don't they?"

He laughed. "Well, there are a few who think that but most of them know you're the tennis coach. They really want to know how you keep the weight off when you're working with all that butter."

Sarah laughed again. "That's my secret."

"You know that I'm here for you," he said as if they were repeating that recent night. She touched his arm this time.

"I know," she said. "I know. But I still don't have any answers."

He nodded and pointed to the room where they were meeting in the Italian restaurant. Before she got in the door, several of her students met her and wanted to introduce her to their parents. Before long, she was surrounded with people who wanted to know more about the cookies. During the banquet itself, she thought how Mark wanted to know about her. It wasn't about the cookies, tennis, or English. It was simply about her. And he didn't care about any difficulty ahead. As he stood in front of the crowd, an ease to his movement speaking in front of them, she was glad he had entered her life. But where they went from there she still didn't know.

Sometimes she broke down and cried. Maybe it was the exhaustion from the school year. Maybe it was her frustration at not knowing what to tell him. Barbara said it meant she was working through another phase of her grief. "I read too many books after my mom died," she would admit, holding out her hand as if it was old news. "But what I mostly did was take my experience and embed it into what I read where it fit."

~ Sisters: The Karma Twist ~

The hardest part of all was the acceptance that Mark would be there for her when she was ready. She didn't believe it. He could find anyone else, she would reason. Then Barbara and Julie would both raise their hands and laugh. "You are such a silly girl. He'll be there."

At the banquet she knew he still was. But she wasn't ready yet. She was moving forward. She wasn't quite there though.

*****

Two years ago, Sarah had been out mowing her grass when a neighbor walking her dog stopped to talk to Sarah.

"You know that the Knights down the street lost their son to…" and with that she inched in closer to Sarah as if to tell her a secret and whispered, "*suicide.*"

Sarah grimaced, gripping her lawnmower handle tighter. Now she knew never to tell Dorothy Mast about Jenna. She thought they might ostracize her from the neighborhood. She stopped her thinking though. That wasn't fair to Jenna. And that wasn't where she let Jenna's death reside.

At Thanksgiving of that year, a piece of paper arrived in her mailbox one afternoon asking everyone to light a strand of purple lights in memory of Greg Knight. Sarah hung two, one for Greg and one for Jenna, a bush on each side of the front door.

On Christmas Eve, a warm one that year for the Midwest, Sarah walked Mairzy through the neighborhood. Strands of purple lights hung on almost every house, even the ones that didn't have other Christmas lights. And the Knight house was lit up with them.

"What I would have given for this," Sarah sighed, standing in front of Greg Knight's house. "The acknowledgement and the support."

Mairzy sniffed a bush in their front yard. Sarah couldn't stop staring, even in the dark night when it was better to be inside with family. Many of the houses they walked by had left the front windows open and Sarah could see the parties going on inside. Part of her missed that in her own life. She missed being a part of events like that. Theirs had changed after Jenna died.

*****

~ Sisters: The Karma Twist ~

Frank and Arlene McCall stopped returning to Chicago. Matt and Donna took their kids to Florida once a year. "It's cheaper than staying at a hotel," Matt would say, shrugging his shoulders, "if I want to take them to that mouse and castle deal."

They begged Sarah to visit them again. Sarah would promise only she'd never make it.

"It's not like you don't have the time," Arlene would say on the phone while Sarah wrinkled her nose on the other end. "You don't teach in the summer."

And what if Jenna was still alive? What if the bakery had happened? Wouldn't they come visit? Wouldn't they want to see what their daughters were up to? But now it was just Sarah left and they didn't find it important. Maybe if she had a family it would have been different.

Sarah almost never went back to her hometown, Cedarville. The busy suburb was a hubbub of family activity.

"One of the best places in the country to raise a family," her friend Julie always said when Sarah drove into town to see her.

"So there's no reason for me to move here if I don't have a family," Sarah would tease, letting Julie's kids run circles around her, before she reached the inside of the house.

But for the first time since her parents moved, Sarah took the long way to Julie's house, on a newer side of town. Sarah drove through the old downtown with its quaint antique stores. On that day, there wasn't a cloud in the sky although there was still a bit of spring chill in the air. It was a Sunday in May, Julie's daughter's fifth birthday.

Sarah took a right turn past the downtown and a tree-lined street took her into the subdivision where the former McCall family home stood. It still looked good. The family that bought it took good care of it. Sarah slowed down, forgetting that she looked obvious, and took a good look at what had been. The tree in the front yard she and Jenna had climbed until Jenna fell out of it and had to have stitches. They were forbidden from climbing it again after that. The driveway they roller skated down a million times, wishing it were higher, longer, faster, the street pavement stopping them with its bumpy surface.

And the house itself. A two-story traditional home. Sarah's bedroom was on the left side of the house, facing the front yard. Jenna's was in the back, just next to Sarah's. But seeing that it was their old house wasn't as painful as remembering that last morning after the papers had been signed and the keys given away. While Sarah knew it wasn't their house anymore and it didn't feel like their house anymore, it was still sad as she watched her parents fill the car with the final few things from the house, whatever they had chosen to take to Florida with them. A lamp that had been in the family for fifty years, her dad's tool kit that he always was afraid to be without, a sculpture Jenna had made in tenth grade that sat on the mantle. All the things they were afraid would break or to be without even temporarily.

They hugged Sarah goodbye and she climbed in her car, parked on the street, and watched them pull out of the driveway of 116 Cedar Lane for the final time. That's what got Sarah. It was one more final time. Just like the last time she saw Jenna. The finality of the end of Jenna's life as they knew it when her casket was lowered into the earth at the cemetery that day. Life was full of final times.

She teared up as they headed down the street, both waving an arm out the window at her. When they disappeared around the corner after the stop sign, she took one last look and drove away. This trip to Julie's was her first time back to the house. In her few visits back to Cedarville, she stayed away, purposely avoiding the house.

Later, when she left Julie's house, the noise of the family and friends behind, she climbed into her silent car and thought about Mark. Instead of heading toward the tollway and going home, Sarah thought she'd make two stops as long as she was there. Driving back toward downtown, she saw the church steeple rise above the buildings in front of her. Sarah parked next to the school and walked across the street, at first stopping to remember the small butcher shop that stood across the street from the church.

It was there that she and Jenna, and her friend Stephanie, used to stop on their way to CCD from their elementary school to buy candy. Sarah smiled, remembering how grown up they felt being left on their own to walk somewhere from their school. And to buy a package of something they would then sit on the concrete church steps and share with each other.

The doors to the church were open, letting the bright sunlight peek in on the dark wood. It was as if a sense of hope made its way inside the old building. Sarah smiled as she felt the wood floors creak under her sandals. She sighed, admitting to herself that it was one of her favorite noises. It brought more comfort than any thought of God could.

It was the first time Sarah had lit a candle for Jenna since the baptism of Julie's son several years ago. She realized she had changed since she'd been in the church last. She didn't feel the anger like she had back then. As she sat in a pew and reflected on everything though, she couldn't help but wonder why the things in life that tore people away from their faith are the same things that make people stronger in their faith?

She knew she had the answer. It was about the struggle. Sometimes it was struggle that made people believe in something. There was a part of Sarah that felt conflicted about this though. If it was struggle that made people eventually come closer to their faith, why did that even have to happen? Was it about greater appreciation of what one has? She sighed again. Sarah wished it hadn't been so difficult. And still she wished it hadn't been so difficult for Jenna.

Sarah began to wish someone sat next to her. She wondered what it would be like to discuss this with someone. She knew that ten years ago she didn't get it. She was too angry. No, angry wasn't the word although it came off that way. She was too hurt. She was too hurt to discuss it with Ken. He was a good person but she wasn't in a place to give him what he needed or what he deserved so she had opened the door to let someone else in for him. That was fair. They never would have made it.

Whether Sarah liked it or not, she wasn't the same person she was when Jenna died. That was to be expected because she was just twenty-two that year. There was still a lot of change in her life. But with each passing year she felt herself ease into different directions of what life taught her, about what was important in life.

And here she was alone in the big church. She realized she didn't have to be. She smiled as she walked back into the sunshine and drove to Jenna's grave. There wasn't the sense of panic as she felt in years past. This time it was a sense of peace and she just needed to be with Jenna for a moment in some way, any way, and the only way she knew how was to drive to the cemetery and sit by her grave, just as they might have done as sisters if one of their parents had died early.

The grass in the cemetery was finally turning green. Sarah hesitated to sit on it because it was still dry but plopped herself down in her miniskirt anyway. She was going home from there. Grass stains or no grass stains.

To see the inscription on Jenna's grave stone– her name, the dates she lived, and "daughter, sister, friend" always brought Sarah a sense of finality. Just like when her parents left the house for the final time.

"Hey girl," Sarah said softly as she sat there. "It's been awhile since I've been here. But I know you aren't really here although I'm not sure where you are."

She ran her fingers across Jenna's name on the gray stone. "It's been kind of a weird time. I know it's been ten years. I know that I should be in a different place than I am. I know that I should have followed what society told me and gotten married and had kids. But I couldn't do it at the time. I don't know if it's too late. I don't know what the future holds. I just couldn't do any of it without you here."

A few cars drove into the cemetery. Sarah wiped her tears and hoped no one came near her. Realizing that was irrational, it was a cemetery after all, she let them begin to fall again. She didn't have to talk to anyone if she didn't want to.

Sitting there, Sarah realized for the first time that Jenna was with her. She couldn't explain what made her sense it. She had no idea where it came from. It almost was as if the idea just popped in her head with large neon lettering to tell her so she didn't miss it. Jenna was with her no matter where she was. Jenna urged her on, jumping around as she usually did. Even when she feared her own future, the demons she was scared to tell anyone about, she still urged Sarah on. Because she knew that Sarah would be okay. She knew that Sarah was the stronger of the two of them. And she knew that Sarah could make their dream happen even if it had changed for her.

Why didn't Jenna give herself a chance? That made Sarah the most sad to think about. Why didn't she realize there was help? The entire family would have supported her and helped her through whatever it was that she thought was happening to her.

"I'm sorry, Jenna," Sarah finally said. "I feel like we let you down. You know we didn't mean to. None of us. We didn't know what you were going through."

~ Sisters: The Karma Twist ~

And at that moment, Sarah also realized she had done everything she could for her sister. There was no more reason to carry her sense of guilt that she had missed something that could have saved Jenna. Ten years was much too long to be carrying any emotions like that, Jenna would have told her, get on with it. And Sarah knew she needed to. She wished she could hug her sister, instead settling for running her fingers across the letters on the grave stone again.

As she did it, a warm breeze enveloped Sarah. She looked up and around, seeing no one there. And no movement in the cemetery. It was Jenna. "Thank you," she whispered.

CHAPTER 29

"Okay," Barbara said, sitting down after she opened the second bottle of wine. She tipped the bottle toward Sarah's glass and Sarah used her hand to push Barbara away.

"No way," she said. "My head isn't clear without any wine these days. That glass was enough to keep me fogged for several days the way I'm going."

"More for me," Barbara shrugged jokingly, pouring some into her own glass. "Anyway, here's the deal." She placed the bottle back on the table and stared at Sarah who sat directly across from her. "Stop the drama. Everything isn't about you. We all have our own issues. God knows I have mine."

"Yeah, I know," Jeff called from the kitchen.

"I didn't ask for your unsolicited opinion," Barbara called back before turning her attention back to Jenna. "No more drama. Cut the drama."

Sarah's lip quivered. She could feel it. Barbara was right and that's what made her lip quiver. It wasn't about the past anymore. It was about freeing herself from the past so she could have the future she deserved. And it was time to do that.

"It's hard for me to let myself be vulnerable with him," she told her friend. "That's part of the reason I still haven't contacted him. I've never let anyone see it. It's like having to completely change a behavior."

Barbara shrugged. "Then that's what you do. You change your behavior."

Sarah laughed, reaching for the wine glass. "You make it sound so easy."

"I've been married for eight years now," she said tilting her head toward the kitchen and reaching for her own wine glass. "He's seen everything about me."

"But he sees me as this strong woman," Sarah tried to explain. "I coach tennis, I teach English. How do you let a man who sees you whack tennis balls against a wall see you in tears?"

Barbara laughed. "You have balls, girl, but that doesn't mean that sometimes you can't shed them for awhile."

"And something else," Barbara said. Sarah almost hated what was next. What was Barbara going to tell her now? "I did some reading up on those pre-birth karma agreement things."

Sarah looked at her friend, sifting through her mental files and not finding one that matched.

"Are you talking about the kama sutra?" Jeff called from the kitchen. Barbara shook her head, reaching behind her and fumbling through the papers.

"That's just you wishing for some sex tonight," she called back, finding what she was looking for. Sitting back down at the table, she said to Sarah, "I looked online and found some information for you."

"I still don't know what you're talking about," Sarah said, feeling a little stupid.

"Don't you remember? The reading at Julie's house?"

Sarah opened her mouth and shut it. "I put that out of my mind. That was like eight months ago."

"Yeah, well, I didn't. I think there's a lot of stuff that will make sense when you start reading," Barbara said, pushing the papers across the table. "You can read it in the bathtub tonight."

"I don't take a bath, you know that. I don't have time. The shower was invented for someone like me."

"Well, then leave it for Mairzy to read and give you a report tomorrow," Barbara suggested. "I've read it all and I'm going to quiz you on it later. And don't forget, no drama!"

Reluctantly, Sarah took the papers home with her. She crawled into her bed, Mairzy at her feet, and started to read. The introduction. The idea that people make agreements with other souls before entering this life.

Or the agreements people make to suffer in this life to learn lessons, to teach others.

Sarah finished reading and dropped the papers on the carpeted floor below her as she turned out the light. Could it be that she and Jenna had a pre-birth agreement? Jenna died so she, Sarah, could help others? To advance both of their souls? Was this karma her teaching others? This was what she was supposed to do? But what about the bakery? How did that figure into this? Sarah couldn't think anymore, letting her mind drift off into another place. Anything was possible, she knew. And with each passing day, she knew she believed it a little more.

*****

The only sound Sarah loved more than the whack of the tennis ball against the court (or a wall) was the crack of the bat at a baseball game. And it was this she thought about on an August morning as she hit the balls against the only solid walls of the group of tennis courts where she coached. It was only 7:30 am. As much as she wanted her girls to show up then, before the sun beat down on the courts at 10:00 am, it was hard to lure them out of bed before 8:00 am. Instead, she was there by herself. She'd woken up restless and it felt good to send the familiar yellow green balls flying into the wall.

"You're out here early," a familiar voice called from the other side of the tall chain link fence. Sarah stopped, resting her hands on her knees for a moment, then looked up to see Mark in shorts and a Falcons baseball shirt standing there watching her. Picking up her water bottle, she walked over to him.

"Hi," she said, wiping her forehead, making sure that her tennis skirt was at least straightened out.

"Having a good summer?" he asked.

"Sure. You?" Sarah took a drink.

"Summer is always good."

Sarah didn't know what to say. What was there to say? Why did he keep trying?

"How's your friend abandonment treating you?" he asked, a slight smile on his face.

~ Sisters: The Karma Twist ~

Sarah tried to smile back.

Mark looked around for a moment and then right at her, his eyes squinting in the sun that was too high for her body to shield. "I really want to take you out. You know that three strikes and you're out but I'm willing to bet I can get a home run if you'd just say yes."

Sarah hoped her face didn't fall. She wanted to retreat back to whacking the balls. How could she explain how deep the scars ran?

"I have tickets to the Cubs game tomorrow night. I really would like you to go to with me."

She shook her head. She could picture Jenna standing next to her, jumping up and down. "Goooo!" she would yell like a cheerleader. "Gooooo!"

Sarah smiled lightly. "Okay. What time do you want to pick me up?"

Mark smiled. "I knew you wouldn't let me strike out. At 4:00."

*****

The date. She finally would go on a date. And with Mark Lennon. "Thank God," Barbara said. "You're lucky he still wants to go out with you." Jenna would have been happy. The night before, Sarah sat in her bedroom staring into her closet. She felt like she was back in high school. What would she wear? Why did it really matter anyway? He saw her everyday at school. And why was she thinking about it a full twenty-four hours before the date?

Mairzy laid by her side, snoozing happily. Sarah touched his head. "Finally, huh?" she asked. Life had changed a lot in ten years. Sarah knew it was time to put things in a different perspective. It wasn't bad, it was just different. It didn't mean she was leaving Jenna behind. It had nothing to do with that. It was time for her to live her life without the shadow of the fear that she let Jenna's death (and what led to it) create in her own life.

Sarah thought about all the years she and Jenna shared. One of the tennis girls had asked her if she ever regretted even having a sister since they only had such a short time together. "No," Sarah had said, "I'm grateful for what we did have." And now she knew that Jenna was with her. It was just different. Again, not bad, just different.

Those women in that support group she had attended, they had been raised that when someone died, the attachment was broken. They were told they had to let the person go to move on. These women didn't want to go on. They were afraid that meant they would lose the memories of their children who had died. They feared it meant a whole chunk of their lives, a very important chunk, would be axed out of their memory.

No one, Sarah finally realized, takes away the memories or the life of a loved one. She didn't understand that herself for a long time. She didn't want to be like those women in the group, yet she couldn't figure out how to let it go. She knew that the bond wasn't broken between Jenna and her. It had changed. She wished someone had told her that a long time ago. Sarah felt like she had missed out on ten years where she still could have felt her sister's presence in her own life.

There was no dwelling on the past though. It wasn't worth it. Time to enjoy the future in front of her and that would begin with Mark Lennon.

When Sarah got up from her bed a photo of her and Jenna caught her eye. She picked it up off her dresser. It was Matt's wedding where they wore the ugly puffy dresses. But their arms were wrapped around each other.

"You two always did get along so well overall," their mother often commented when she looked at photos of them.

Sarah touched her sister's face. She wondered if in some way they both knew their time together was short, that they only would have those seventeen or so years together and they had to make the most of them. But if they knew that, why did they make future plans? That part didn't make sense.

There was still a lot that didn't make sense to Sarah. She knew someday it would, but not now from where she was standing. And she just hoped that when that day came, Jenna would be there to greet her and help her understand it all. No, she knew Jenna would be there. "Took you long enough," her sister would joke. And Sarah wouldn't be mad at her for cutting her own life short anymore. She couldn't be. Jenna had no idea what her death would mean to all of them. All she could think of was her own fear. And pain.

Sarah put the photo down and left the room with Mairzy trailing behind. Some day, she thought, I'll get it, but for now I have to let it go. Whatever the pre-birth karma agreement is.

~ Sisters: The Karma Twist ~

*****

Sarah paced her front hall for at least fifteen minutes waiting for Mark to pick her up. At least no one would ever know, except Mairzy who followed her every move, how nervous she was. She picked up the racket in the hallway and bounced a ball under it.

"Hi," Mark said, when Sarah opened the door. "We're still on for tonight, right?"

Sarah laughed, dropped the racket and the ball, and shut the door behind her.

It would be her first trip to Wrigley Field since Jenna's death. She and Jenna had been there the last summer of Jenna's life. A night game, just like this one, Sarah thought, as they walked into the twinkling lights of Wrigley Field. A warm, early summer night.

That had been a significant night although not necessarily a happy one for them. Jenna had been mad at Sarah for hanging out on the concourse for part of the game. "I can't believe you went out there instead of sitting here with me," Jenna had complained when Sarah returned. "Stupid boys."

Sarah never told Jenna what transpired on the concourse. Any other day she knew her sister would have been happy for her, that Don Rogers, one of the boys she dated in high school, had been out there, and he'd kissed Sarah when he saw her. Until Jenna's death, Sarah held out hope that maybe she and Don might still date. After Jenna died, she never thought of him again, her grief taking over all those empty spots in her brain.

She knew Jenna was mad that night, her arms crossed in front of her chest, that it wasn't worth telling her sister. Instead, Jenna sulked most of the night and they never returned to Wrigley after that.

Taking a deep breath, Sarah walked through the gates of the ballpark, Mark right behind her. Tonight, she told herself, tonight will be different.

And it was. For the first time, she felt a strength being with Mark. Was it there all along and she hadn't allowed it to happen? Or was it because she had been so afraid to let go of her sister, afraid because she didn't believe anything could replace her sadness for Jenna's death, that it wouldn't let Mark's presence flow through to her? She reached over and put her hand on top of Mark's. He smiled, then reached over and kissed her on the cheek.

~ Sisters: The Karma Twist ~

CHAPTER 30

Sarah looked around her before she began her talk for the fall athletes. She knew Jenna was with her. Though she had her doubts through the years, they weren't there tonight. She'd learned many lessons since February. "Be with me, Jenna," she whispered, "be with me."

And with that, she began with her sister's story. Sarah knew Jenna wasn't an anomaly. Looking around at the student-athletes in front of her, any one of them could be a Jenna. Probably there was more than one Jenna in the room.

"You got it," she could hear Jenna saying. "Took you ten years to figure out what you were supposed to do. I couldn't help you though. I had to let you walk that road to get where you could understand it. Now take it and run with it."

Maybe this is what that karma agreement was about. Maybe this was what she had to learn to get to that relationship.

*****

"You decided to give her a voice," Mark said, walking up to her after the last student asked questions or made comments.

Sarah nodded, slipping out of her heels. "Someone I know suggested that I do it. Took me all summer to mull it over though."

They walked outside, Sarah holding her shoes in her hands until they reached the outside pavement where she put them back on. The wind picked up from a storm rolling in. When they reached Sarah's car, Mark stopped and waited for her to unlock it. She could tell he wasn't in a hurry to leave. She wanted to tell him that she didn't want him to leave. Instead, they stood there in the dark under the school's parking lot lights.

"It's like we're students," she said. "I feel like I should tell you I need to go home or I'll be in trouble."

"And I need to tell you that I'll see you in first period tomorrow," Mark said with a smile back.

The wind whipped Sarah's hair back onto her face and she dug in her bag for a hair band to tie it back. She loved that she felt love in the present moment of her life. She didn't miss Jenna. She knew Jenna was with her. She didn't have that longing to be elsewhere, to be someone else, to wonder what life would have been like. If only. Those thoughts were gone.

"I'm glad you didn't forget I was waiting for you," he said.

Sarah didn't know what to say. She didn't know what to feel. Her mouth felt dry like it didn't work. Finally she said, "No matter where the journey takes you, you have to travel it." She wasn't sure if he waited for her to add something else.

"As long as it takes me wherever you are," he said, wrapping his arms around her. Sarah let herself be present in his arms.

"It was a journey back to life," she said, silently adding "and love."

And she knew Jenna would be proud. Sarah could picture exactly what she would say, "I told you to keep this one. Thank God you finally listened to your little sister for once. Took you long enough."